Murder in Oakwood Park
A Rebecca Snow Cozy Mystery

Jane T. O'Brien

This book is fiction. All characters, events, and organizations portrayed in this novel are the product of the author's imagination or are used fictitiously. Any resemblance to actual persons –living or dead—is entirely coincidental.

Mystery Series by Jane T. O'Brien

Samantha Degan Cozy Mystery Series
Murder in Stonehill Manor
Murder in Lancashire
Murder in Ashville
Murder at Seabrook Shores
Murder at Pepperberry Lake (a short story)

Molly Ryan Cozy Mystery Series
Murder in Hillsboro
Murder in Kincaid Towers
Murder in Evergreen
Murder at Coventry Hill Inn

Cassandra Cross Cozy Mystery Series
Murder on The Isabella
Murder at Channel Two
Murder in Newcastle
Murder at Cranberry Creek

Rebecca Snow Cozy Mystery Series
Murder in Oakwood Park
Murder on Bradbury Hill
Murder on Applewood Circle
Murder at Lake Willoughby

Avery Snow Cozy Mystery Series
Murder in Somerset County
Murder in Hidden Oaks
Murder on Ravenwood Campus
Murder in Clearview Park

Katie McDougal Cozy Mystery Series
Murder in Brookhaven
Murder in Rosedale Hospital
Murder at Driftwood Bay

Other Books by Jane T. O'Brien

Novels
Bristol Falls
Glenwood Hills
Cumberland Heights

Cozy Mysteries
Murder in Forest Glen
The Mystery of Shelby Lake
The Mystery of Waverly Island
Murder in Pinewood Bluff

Camden Corners Collection
Camden Corners Book One
Camden Corners Book Two
Camden Corners Book Three

Children's Books

Finian Frog Series
Fabulous Finian Frog
Finian Frog Falls in Love
Finian Frog and Farley's Wishes
Finian Frog and Froglet Freddy

Hennessey Hound Tales Series
Happy Hennessey Hound

Prologue

"Rebecca, thank heaven you're at home. I need you," cried Carolina Bloom in her overly dramatic way.

"Carolina, calm down, nothing is as bad as you seem to think. Tell me what you need from me."

"They're going to replace *Carolina Bloom in the Morning* with an old sitcom if I can't get someone to fill in for me while I recover from the flu. I told them you would do it."

"Fill in for you; Carolina, why me? Hosting a live television show is out of the question; isn't there someone with experience who a better choice would be?"

"Rebecca, you are wonderful in the dramas at the Oakwood Park Community Playhouse. I'm desperate. If I can't find someone by tomorrow morning's show, I'm done."

***

Thus, began Rebecca Snow's career in local television. Carolina's flu continued while Rebecca hosted her show.

Those who knew Carolina tried to convince her to see a doctor for the lingering effects of her illness that kept her down and feeling dreadful.

Although she knew it was temporary, Rebecca enjoyed hosting the show. She never called it her show, always reminding the audience that she was filling in for the one and only Carolina Bloom.

On a Sunday morning, Andy Snow placed the Oakwood Park Chronicle on the kitchen table without noticing the headline. Rebecca filled his cup with freshly brewed coffee, and while pouring her own, glanced at the front page of the paper.

LOCAL TALK SHOW HOSTESS
DEAD AT FORTY-FIVE

Carolina Bloom, popular local entertainer and hostess of *Carolina Bloom in the Morning* has died after a lingering illness. An autopsy is scheduled to determine the cause of death. Foul play is a possibility.

Chapter One

Rebecca Snow is a forty-something empty nester living with her husband, Andy, in the home they have shared since they returned from their honeymoon over twenty years ago.

Rebecca is the youngest of five daughters born to Susan and Mitch Wilson and the last of the Wilson girls to marry.

Each wedding had taken a toll on Susan and Mitch financially as well as physically.

"Rebecca, we will give you a large wedding if that's what you and Andrew want, or you can have the money as a down payment on a home of your own."

Rebecca and Andy didn't have to think about it. They began looking for a house the very next day and found the home of their dreams.

***

Now that the children are grown and on their own, Rebecca and Andy talk about moving to a smaller place, but it never goes further than talk.

In high school, Rebecca was a member of the drama club along with her classmate, Carolina Bloom. Rebecca caught the acting bug and often fantasized about being a movie star. Carolina, however, had more talent than Rebecca and her fantasy was more apt to come true.

After graduation, Rebecca went to the local University where she met Andrew Snow, the two were inseparable and Rebecca knew she would never leave her hometown or Andy. Carolina enrolled in acting school and soon realized the competition in New York was greater than in Oakwood Park Senior High School.

For the next few years, Carolina was cast in minor roles in plays on and off Broadway. She met Gavin Lancaster, a fellow actor. They married three weeks after their first meeting. Life was good for Gavin and Carolina although they lived on a shoestring. They continually auditioned together and separately and most often were cast in non-speaking or bit parts. Six months after they vowed to love each other forever, Gavin was offered a part as a leading man in a new play on Broadway. The couple celebrated over champagne, a rare treat for them. Unfortunately, the play closed shortly after the opening, but not before Gavin fell in love with his leading lady.

Carolina was crushed, she had dreams they would one day move to California and become the most famous couple Hollywood had ever seen.

***

The would-be Broadway sensation returned to Oakwood Park to think about her life choices. After receiving little sympathy from her mother who thought acting was a waste of time, Carolina sought out her old friend Rebecca.

***

"I wish I could settle for a life like yours, Rebecca. Don't you wonder what it would be like if you'd followed your dream instead of spending your days dusting furniture and changing diapers?"

Rebecca didn't recall having a dream she wanted to follow but didn't think it was worth arguing with her former classmate. Her life was full, she actually enjoyed being home with her baby. She didn't mind housework and loved to cook and bake for Andy.

"Carolina, if you are planning to stay in Oakwood Park, you should check out the new Community Playhouse. It's scheduled to open in a couple of months."

"Community Playhouse? It sounds like a bunch of amateurs. You forget I'm a professional, it would be disastrous if I lowered my standards by joining with no-talent locals."

Rebecca held her tongue and didn't remind Carolina that although she was a professional, she was an out-of-work professional.

"Maybe you should try again in New York or California, a break in your acting career could be just around the corner."

Carolina listened to her friend's encouraging words and decided to try Hollywood again.

Two months later, Carolina met Milton Harrington, a successful director. She was cast in a film as a schoolteacher who becomes the victim of a serial killer. She was only on screen for the better part of four minutes but landed the role of Milton Harrington's wife.

Carolina's happiness was short-lived when she discovered Milton wanted to direct every aspect of her life.

After years of misery in her marriage, she found Milton collapsed on the marble kitchen floor suffering from an apparent heart attack. He died before the paramedics arrived and left Carolina a rich widow.

Carolina quickly learned money could get her the parts she felt she deserved. For the next fifteen years, she had parts in several unexceptional movies.

Eventually, Milton's money ran low. Carolina was nearing forty and although the surgeon had removed the signs of age, she knew her career wasn't producing the success of her dreams. She remembered Rebecca Snow mentioning some silly community playhouse in Oakwood Park. It had been years since the opening, would it still be around? There was only one way to find out. She'd place a call to her good friend, Rebecca.

***

"Carolina Bloom, is it really you after all these years? Andy and I have seen many of your movies." She didn't mention how mediocre the movies were. "Your mother is very proud of you, she can't stop talking about her daughter, the movie star."

"My mother talks about my acting career? That's a switch. How is the old bat, I haven't spoken to her since I left town years ago?"

"Oh dear, I didn't realize you and your mother are estranged, I'm sorry to hear that."

"Don't be! I'm calling to see if the local playhouse is still in existence. It was about to open when I visited with you before I made it big in Hollywood."

Rebecca winced at Carolina's words. Everyone knew she'd married a much older man and when he died, he left her a bundle.

"Yes, Carolina, the theater is very popular; why do you ask?"

"I was thinking of coming back to Oakwood Park for an extended visit. I thought I could lend my talents to the community."

"I'm sure you would be welcome although we are only a community theater, nothing like the Broadway productions and Hollywood creations you are accustomed to."

"It sounds like you are a part of the theater, Rebecca, did the acting bug bite you again?"

"I guess you could say that. When the children were young, I worked behind the scenes, now that they are grown and I have more time on my hands, I do act when they need me."

"How fun," Carolina responded in a condescending tone. "I'll be in town on Tuesday, set up a meeting with whoever's in charge, don't make it too early, I don't do mornings."

Rebecca couldn't imagine what was behind Carolina's interest in the Oakwood Park Community Playhouse.

Before she hung up, Carolina said, "By the way, Rebecca, I hear Brad Pickett is coming to town to sell his mama's house."

Rebecca's mouth dropped open. Brad was coming to Oakwood Park. He didn't come home when his father died five years before and didn't show up for his mother's funeral six months ago. He'd hired the local funeral home to plan for both services.

Rebecca's face burned as she remembered her humiliation thanks to Brad Pickett years before.

Chapter Two

Prom was the only thing Rebecca Wilson, and her friends could talk about for weeks. They'd planned for this special day since the Christmas break. The prom was held three weeks before graduation.

Rebecca was dating Brad Pickett, the handsome captain of the football team. She found herself doodling **Mrs. Bradley Pickett**, in her notebook pages as she dreamed of her wedding day. "I'm the luckiest girl in the world," she would tell her friends; never noticing the skepticism that showed in their eyes.

Rebecca found the perfect prom dress, her sisters helped with her make-up and hair. Her mother and father both had tears in their eyes as they watched their youngest daughter glide down the stairs like a princess.

Brad arrived looking handsome in his tuxedo, he placed a corsage on her wrist, and she pinned a boutonnière in his lapel. Rebecca finally had to tell them to stop taking pictures or they would never make it to the dance.

Mr. Wilson reminded Brad that Rebecca must be home no later than two o'clock in the morning. The look on his face told Brad he expected him to act like a gentleman the entire evening.

***

Rebecca was having a wonderful time dancing and laughing with their friends. The band played a number everyone liked, and they all got up from the table to dance. Rebecca was left by herself wondering where Brad could have gone.

After what seemed to be an eternity, her friend, Stephanie, told her date to check the men's room, thinking Brad might be ill.

"He's not in there, Rebecca," said Adam Reynolds. "I checked outside, and his car is gone."
"

Rebecca looked around the table and saw the pity in the eyes of her friends. It was a look of pity but not one of surprise.

"Adam and I will drive you home, Rebecca," said Stephanie.

"No, I'll call a cab, you guys stay and have fun." Rebecca didn't know how much longer she could keep the tears from flowing.

Adam got up, walked around the table, and took Rebecca by the arm. "Let's get you out of here," he said.

Rebecca made it to the front door of her home and fell sobbing into her mother's waiting arms.

***

Rebecca cried herself to sleep that night and the next morning her four sisters greeted her. Each had a story to tell about a mortifying experience they'd had in high school.

***

"Rebecca, we are going to take you to New York City. Mom and Dad have given permission for you to miss school on Thursday and Friday. It will be a pre-exam week vacation."

Rebecca didn't think she wanted to go anywhere or do anything for the rest of her life, but her sisters were so excited, she smiled and said it sounded like fun.

That afternoon, her friends came to see her to offer sympathy and tell her the jerk wasn't good enough for her. The pain of a broken romance was still there but it helped to have understanding friends and family. The one person she didn't hear from was Bradley Pickett.

Monday came and she had to force herself to go to school. Being dumped was one thing, but being dumped in front of the entire senior class was agonizing. She passed Brad in the hall, he looked sheepish but said nothing.

***

The Wilson girls left for New York City. Rebecca's sisters always made her laugh, she'd all but forgotten Brad and the disastrous prom. They saw the sights of the city, shopped in the stores on Fifth Avenue and watched the Today show from the street. Al Roker interviewed them on live television. Susan Wilson taped the show in case they made it on. When the sisters returned to Oakwood Park, Rebecca invited her friends to a viewing party, and they watched as she announced to the world that she and her sisters were in New York to celebrate her being dumped at prom.

***

Her friends thought Rebecca was a natural in front of a camera and said she should show the tape at graduation. They all laughed uproariously at the thought.

***

Thinking back to that time put a smile on Rebecca's face. Most of her friends from high school had gone off to college but returned to Oakwood Park to marry, settle down and start their families. Rebecca was happy she wasn't married to Bradley Pickett, but couldn't help but hope, after all these years, he was overweight and bald.

***

Stephanie and Adam are still together and the parents of three. Adam is mayor of Oakwood Park and Rebecca still remembers the way he took care of her the night of prom.

"He's a great guy, Stephanie, you are lucky to have him."

"Your Adam will come along, Rebecca,"

Stephanie was right. Her Adam came in the form of Andy Snow.

***

Rebecca had succeeded in putting prom night out of her mind through the years, but it suddenly occurred to her that she hadn't seen Carolina Bloom on the dance floor after Brad disappeared. All those years ago. and now she was figuring out who was with Brad. *Carolina, you traitor, I'll have to remember to thank you when I see you again.*

Chapter Three

Rebecca's cell phone sounded as she was about to leave her house.

"Rebecca, you'll never guess who is in town, Brad Pickett," said Mary Lou Franklin, a former classmate who a real estate agent is now.

"I heard he was in town, Mary Lou, I hope you have the listing for Mrs. Pickett's house. It's a beautiful home, it should sell quickly."

"Yes, it's my listing but it's in need of repairs. Brad ignored his mother's house as well as ignoring his mother. He wants me to sell it 'as is' so he can get back to civilization, as he calls it. Gosh, was he always a jerk?"

"Satisfy my curiosity, Mary Lou, is he fat and bald?"

"I wish I could tell you he is ugly, if anything, he improved with age."

"Someone is at my door, Mary Lou, thanks for the information and good luck with the sale." *Saved by the bell*, Rebecca thought, *the last person I want to talk about is Brad Pickett.* She opened the door and recognized Brad Pickett smiling at her.

"Hi Becky, long time no see."

"Hello Bradley," she replied knowing he loathed being called Bradley as much as she disliked the nickname Becky. She had nothing against the name, however, she is named after her grandmother, Rebecca, who she loved dearly.

"You don't seem surprised to see me. Are you going to invite me in?"

"As a matter of fact, I was about to leave when the doorbell rang. It was good to see you but I'm running late for an appointment."

"Come on, you can make time for an old friend."

"I don't mean to be rude, but you leave me no choice," Rebecca began to shut the door when he stuck his foot in to stop her.

"These are five-hundred-dollar shoes you just ruined with that door; it should prove to you how much I want to talk to you."

"Tell me what you came to say and then leave." She stood blocking his way inside the house.

"I came to apologize for leaving the night of prom. It was your old man's fault, you know."

"What are you talking about?" She asked.

"Your old man ruined my plans for the evening when he said he wanted you home by two o'clock. Our friends were pulling all-nighters and you had a curfew."

"I don't remember any of my friends being out all night. What did you plan to do in the wee hours of the morning?"

He smiled at her in such a way it gave her chills. She breathed a sigh of relief when she saw Andy's car pull into the driveway.

***

He came into the kitchen through the garage. "Hi, hon, I came home for the proposal I worked up last night." He stopped when he saw there was someone at the door.

"Hello," he said holding out his hand, "Andy Snow, glad to meet you."
Brad shook Andy's hand. "I'm an old friend of your wife, I'm Brad Pickett. I presume you've heard of me."

Andy knew all about the debacle at Rebecca's prom but didn't let on he'd heard of it.

"Sorry, guy, I know most of Rebecca's friends, your name doesn't sound familiar. You must be from out-of-town.
"Rebecca, aren't you late for your meeting, I thought you'd have left already."

"I should have left ten minutes ago; I made the mistake of answering my phone and then the doorbell rang."

"Goodbye, Bradley, it was nice seeing you again, but I really must go."

Brad didn't like being dismissed; women usually fell for his charms.

***

"Thanks for the fib, Andy. He's a real jerk, he put the blame on my dad for leaving me at the prom. He said he'd planned an all-nighter if you can believe it, and Dad put the kibosh on it when he said I had a two o'clock curfew. I was seventeen years old for heaven sake."

"He is a jerk, but I can see where a young girl could fall for his good looks."

"Hey, Andrew Snow, you aren't a slouch in the good-looks department yourself. If I wasn't already late for this meeting…"

Andy smiled, he'd often wondered about Brad Pickett and how anyone could walk out on a girl like Rebecca. Andy had fallen in love with her the first time he saw her, and that love grew with each passing day and year.

At the Community Playhouse

Rebecca apologized for being late to the meeting of the community players.

"We're glad you're late, Rebecca, it gave us a chance to vote for you to give the bad news to Barry Kemp. He can't play Inspector Turley in our next production."

"Is that my punishment for being late? I'd rather serve popcorn and lemonade at the refreshment stand during the children's matinee."

"I agree," said Sandy Clark, the leader of the volunteer crew. "However, Rebecca, you have such a gentle way of telling our wannabe actors they can't act."

"Yes, Rebecca, folks don't mind getting the heave-ho when you tell them the bad news," Harvey Rutledge said with a chuckle. Harvey a spry eighty-two-year old was the eldest member of the group and a retired high school drama coach.

"On a more pleasant subject," said Rebecca, "Carolina Bloom will be returning to Oakwood Park and is considering offering her talents to our group."

"Carolina can be such a diva. She was bad enough before she became semi-famous. She'd bring in more money than we usually get, but putting up with her might not be worth it," said Sandy.

"What do you think, Rebecca? Do you think she'd fit in with our group? I like being the director and don't want any help from her," said Marsha Brill.

"Marsha, you'll be lucky if she doesn't take over your job and you'll be the one handing out popcorn to the children," said Harvey.

"Why don't we wait until she gets here," said Rebecca. "It could be that she doesn't want to work with amateurs. Let's not ask for trouble before it happens."

"Rebecca," said Elaine Baker, "did you hear Brad Pickett is back in town? His poor mama would be so upset if she knew he'd missed her funeral."

"Yes, I heard, in fact, he is the reason I was late. He showed up at my doorstep uninvited."

"Did you give him a piece of your mind, Rebecca?" Harvey asked.

Was there one person in this entire town who hadn't heard about what happened to her over twenty years ago?

"No, Harvey, believe it or not, I got over that mess a long time ago."

Sandy Clark adjourned the meeting.

"Thank you for talking to Barry, Rebecca, I hope he doesn't give you a hard time."

"I hope not either, Sandy. I think I'll head over to the television station; I might as well get this over as soon as possible."

At the television station

Rebecca was happy Barry Kemp was at the station when she stopped by to see him.

"Hello, Rebecca, are you here to talk about my part as Inspector Turley? I think I nailed the audition."

"Barry, your enthusiasm is refreshing, however, the director doesn't think you are right for the part. I'm sorry to tell you, someone else will play the inspector."

"Is it because I forgot my lines before? I know I could do better. I get nervous when I see all those people in the audience."

"That's understandable, maybe a few small parts would give you more confidence. In the meantime, we can use your help behind the scenes. Sandy is always looking for someone to help with set decoration."

"I'll think about it, I'm too disappointed to volunteer for anything today. You understand, don't you, Rebecca?"

"I understand, Barry," she responded knowing Barry would never have a bigger part than a bystander on set.

"I hear Carolina Bloom is coming to town, maybe she can help me with my lines for the next production."

"Where did you hear that, Barry?" Rebecca asked. She hadn't told anyone about Carolina's plans until today at her meeting.

"Barb Tinsdale, Mr. Carlson's assistant, said Carolina will be here tomorrow. I hope you aren't upset after what happened at prom with Carolina and your date," Barry said sheepishly.

"Barry, I'm married and have two grown children. I'm looking forward to being a grandmother in a few years. I can assure you; I don't dwell on what happened at a high school dance years ago," Rebecca said while saying to herself, *I wouldn't think about prom if people would stop bringing it up.* She did wonder how Barry Kemp knew about Carolina being the one Brad ran off with that night. *Oh well, what does it matter?*

"Sorry, Rebecca, thanks for stopping by to let me down easy, I don't think the others have the nerve to tell me they don't want me in their play."

"Barry, when my kids were small, I did spend some time decorating sets and getting ready for the shows. I enjoyed doing that and it didn't take as much time as acting in a play. Think about it, I'm sure they would welcome your help."

Chapter Four

Meanwhile in the Harrington mansion

Carolina Bloom packed the last of her belongings into a carry-on bag. She stood in the foyer looking up to the glass chandelier in the center of the ceiling with a winding staircase cascading to the floor below. Milton Harrington was a control freak, but he gave fabulous parties in this old mansion. Carolina closed her eyes picturing herself in one of her many lovely gowns. The guests would stare in awe as she glided down the stairs. Milton always greeted her with an approving look.

Caroline knew she was merely a trophy wife. Milton was old enough to be her grandfather and had no interest in her except to impress his cronies.

Lucky for me, he only lived for six years after our marriage. The parties were the only reason I stayed married to the old coot.

Carolina knew the parties weren't the only thing that kept her tied to Milton. Her life was one of ease, she had her own personal assistant to take care of her every need. The chauffeur was at her beck and call allowing her to shop any time she wanted which was often. There was no limit on her credit cards and all the best salesgirls in the posh dress salons catered to her whims.

After Milton's death, his financial manager warned her against making investments without his approval. Carolina wanted to continue the lavish parties but was told it would be disrespectful to give a party or wear anything other than black for a year after Mr. Harrington's death.

"What a stupid rule, I look terrible in black and I have some wonderful ideas for parties. I'll perish if I can't have fun for a whole year."

"I'm certain you won't perish, madam. Remember what I said about investing and you will live well for years to come."

Carolina didn't heed the man's advice. She thought she could become a major figure in the movie industry. She bought her way into starring in or producing one movie after another. Most were forgettable no matter how much money she poured into them.

It wasn't her lack of acting talent as it was her choice of screenplays. She chose roles and scripts that were unsuitable, usually with more sex than substance. She thought of herself as a sex symbol. After all, it was her sex appeal, and willingness, that lured Brad Pickett away from the most popular girl in the senior class. Milton Harrington wouldn't have given her a second look if she'd been plain and flat chested.

For years, her mother berated her for her low grades in school. *'you'd better marry for money, Carolina. Your large bosom is the only thing you have going for you.'* Ida Bloom had no idea how much her words hurt her daughter. Carolina knew her mother resented the invasion of a child on her life. Ida was a single woman in her late forties. She was content with her life and didn't see the need for a man to become a part of it. One day a salesman entered the store. He was a handsome fellow whose sweet talk Ida couldn't ignore. A couple of months after their first meeting Ida found herself in a family way. After breaking the news to the father of her unborn baby, the man said he had no intention of leaving his wife or being a father to Ida's child.

Pride kept Ida from suing the man for child support. She held her head high and announced she was expecting a baby. Although the townspeople were curious about the child's father, everyone was too polite to ask.

Ida never told Carolina anything about her father. The subject was never mentioned. If Carolina was curious about the man, she didn't let on.

All the children in Oakwood Park knew Ms. Bloom, the story lady. Their parents brought them to the bookstore every Wednesday and Friday for story time. Carolina watched as her mother sat on a small stool with children encircling her. She called them all by name as they hugged her after she read them a story.

The children Carolina's ages often told her how lucky she was to have the story lady as her mother. Carolina didn't think she was lucky at all. Her mother was happier when she was with a bunch of kids than she ever was when they were alone. Ida tried to interest her daughter in reading, but the girl refused.

"Mama, why do you like being with other children more than you like being with me?"

"Don't talk nonsense, Carolina, pick up a book and read it instead of badgering me. Your teacher says you should read more. How do you think it looks when the only bookstore owner in Oakwood Park has a daughter who can't read? You and your make-believe, you can't live your life in a fantasy world, Carolina."

Carolina did read but only late at night when Ida was asleep. She wouldn't give her mother the satisfaction of letting her know she enjoyed the lives she read about. They were much more exciting than her own life.

Ida Bloom didn't know how to be a parent. Her own mother was a cold, unfeeling woman who feigned illness when Ida needed her advice and guidance. The woman only knew how to insult and berate her only child.

Ida found it difficult to love the child of the man who'd abandoned her. If only Carolina looked more like her, but she was the image of her father.

Carolina's interest in the drama club alarmed Ida. She watched as Carolina's figure changed from a girl to a teenager. Ida had to admit, her daughter was a beauty with her long blonde hair and stunning figure.

"Carolina, here's a heavy sweater to put over that skimpy shirt. I don't want you giving those boys in the school any ideas. Don't think about acting, those people are evil, it's nothing but sex on the movie screen these days."

"What's wrong, Mama, are you afraid I'll end up like you?"

Carolina felt the sting of her mother's hand on her cheek and vowed she would leave home the day after graduation.

***

Carolina smiled through the graduation ceremony knowing she would be out of Oakwood Park the very next day. With the money she'd swiped from her mother's strongbox, she paid for acting school and had enough for a dreary flat she shared with six other aspiring actors. She didn't like school and hated living with strangers.

Carolina forced herself to stick it out and was rewarded with small roles in Broadway productions. The money she made was not enough to move out of her crowded apartment. She'd been fired from her waitress job because she was a no-show on the days, she had an audition.

"Carolina, I know you are an actress, but I hired you to wait tables. If you can't show up to work, I'll find someone who can."

Carolina's future looked bleak, if she didn't get a break soon, she would be forced to return to Oakwood Park and beg her mother to take her back. She hadn't seen or heard from Ida since the day she left.

The next day, Carolina met Gavin Lancaster. It was love at first sight. Carolina's dreams were finally coming true and her world was looking up until the day Gavin announced he was in love with someone else.

After briefly returning to her hometown, Carolina set her sights on a career in the movies. Again, she left her mother's home with the remaining contents of the hidden strongbox.

Chapter Five

Brad Pickett pulled away from Rebecca's house in his red sports car convertible.

Rebecca is even more beautiful than I remember. If anything, age has improved her looks.

If I hadn't gone off with Carolina that night, I might have been that guy standing by her side. Who am I kidding, I'd go nuts living in this crappy town all my life? I wouldn't be back here now if it weren't for Carolina's threats.

What is it about Carolina Bloom that makes me lose my sanity when I'm around her? Sure, she's hot, but so are plenty of other females whose company I've enjoyed over the years.

What possessed me to tell her about my insider trading scheme? Thanks to my big mouth that night, I could be facing prison time. At the very least, I'd lose my job and be forced to give up the things that make my life worth living.

Bradley Albert Pickett is the only child of Herman and Elsie Pickett. His parents doted on the boy from the moment he was born. With his dark curly hair and sparkling grey-blue eyes, he attracted attention from the Pickett neighbors and friends. When he reached his teen years, he was the type young girls swooned over. Although Brad had known Rebecca Wilson since kindergarten, the two became inseparable in their high school years. That is, until the night of the prom when Brad left Rebecca alone to go off with the willing Carolina Bloom.

After graduation, Brad left Oakwood Park for college and never planned to return. Upon hearing of his father's death, he told his mother that he couldn't break away from his job, the brokerage firm didn't allow for bereavement leave. It wasn't true but as usual, Elsie didn't doubt her son's words.

Two years later, a neighbor informed Brad that his mother had died. He called the local funeral home, and they handled her burial.

Brad hadn't seen Carolina Bloom since their high school graduation. One day, as he was walking to the local delicatessen, he heard his name being called. Brad turned and saw the smiling face of Carolina Bloom.

"Carolina, is that you? I'd know that sexy face anywhere," he said glancing at her chest.

"My face is up here," Carolina said pointing up, "Brad Pickett, you haven't changed a bit, you're still the same degenerate you were back in high school."

They continued seeing each other when Carolina came to New York or Brad found an excuse to visit California. It wasn't a serious relationship; they both enjoyed the time they spent together but never talked about the future.

Brad's mistake came one day over a year ago. He'd felt particularly proud of an insider trading deal he'd made that morning. He and Carolina celebrated with a bottle of expensive scotch.

Carolina was never much of a drinker but coaxed Brad to have another and another. She knew he was holding back some important information and was determined to urge him to spill the beans.

Brad complied, he bragged about how he'd overheard a private conversation and acted upon it. He would stand to make a lot of money. What he didn't know was that Carolina had recorded his every word.

The next morning Brad awoke with the worst hangover he'd ever remembered. Carolina was asleep with a smile on her face.

I don't remember, but I must have been really good last night.

Brad's inflated ego had no idea Carolina was smiling because of the many ways she was planning to blackmail him with his own words.

Carolina had no intention of profiting monetarily from her newfound knowledge. No, she had other plans for him. It was always good publicity when a movie star had a handsome escort by her side. She knew the time would come when her looks began to fade. It wasn't fair that men looked better with age whereas women tended to simply look old. Brad might not be willing to continue their liaisons unless he had an incentive. Staying out of prison was a good one.

The day after Carolina returned to California, she called Brad.

"Hi, beautiful, did you forget something when you left my apartment."

"No, Brad, I took something with me, something very entertaining." She told him to listen while she played his words back to him confessing his insider trading.

Brad seethed with anger. She'd tricked him, plied him with scotch and coerced him into a confession.

No, it wasn't a confession, I was bragging about my brilliant move.

"Carolina, if you were here, I'd wring your scrawny neck."

"That's why I returned to California before sharing the tape with you. Don't think about getting rid of me, Brad. I made a copy of the tape and it's in my lawyer's office. I've instructed him to play the tape if something suspicious happens to me."

"How much do you want, Carolina?"

"I'm not after your money, Brad, at least, not yet. I'm only asking that I have your attention when I need it. You're a handsome man, Brad, you will make a perfect escort for me."

Brad slammed the phone down. He vowed never to allow a drop of scotch to cross his lips in the future. He would do as Carolina asked but he would resent every minute of it.

***

Months passed before Brad heard from Carolina.

"Brad, it's time to pay up. It seems dear old Milton's money has all but dried up." She didn't add that she was the one who spent Milton's fortune.

"Now, you want my money. How much to keep that scheming mouth shut?"

"Keep that in mind, Brad. For now, I want you to meet me in Oakwood Park. If I'm forced to return to that wretched town, I want to go back victorious. Tongues will wag when I show up with Rebecca Wilson's favorite lover on my arm."

"Rebecca and I were never lovers, Carolina, don't you remember that's why I hooked up with you?"

"I don't remember hearing you complain at the time. You know I'm much more of a woman than Rebecca ever was."

Brad ignored her words; he didn't want to talk about Rebecca with Carolina. His pulse raced thinking about the girl he'd betrayed.

What a fool I was, Rebecca Wilson was the best thing that ever happened to me and I blew it. All those years ago, my mother couldn't wait to tell me Rebecca was getting married to a wonderful young man.

Elsie Pickett realized she and Herman were responsible for Bradley's behavior. The Picketts had given up hope of having a child of their own when Elsie began feeling queasy every morning. Thinking she had a stomach virus; she visited her doctor after two weeks passed and she wasn't feeling better.

"Elsie, you have been feeling sick, not because of an illness," Dr. Wolfe exclaimed, "you and Herman are about to become parents."

Elsie burst into tears.

"Marie," Dr. Wolfe called to his nurse, "have Mr. Pickett come in, please."

Elsie cried uncontrollably, Dr. Wolfe had seen a variety of reactions when he informed his patients of their pregnancy, but never anything like this.

"Elsie, please calm down, I thought you would be pleased with the news."

A worried Herman was alarmed when he walked through the exam room door to find Elsie dissolved in tears.

"What's wrong with her, Dr. Wolfe, is her condition serious?"

"Would you like to tell Herman the news, Elsie or should I tell him?"

"You tell," she managed to say.

"Herman, I can assure you Elsie is perfectly healthy, her condition is normal for a woman who is expecting a baby."

Herman's mouth flew open and when he was able to speak, he said, "It can't be! Elsie, did you hear what the doctor said? You're going to have a baby." He wrapped his arms around his wife and they both sobbed.

Dr. Wolfe left the room, giving the couple some time to absorb the shock of being parents after all these years.

Throughout the next seven months, Elsie did everything the doctor told her to do to make sure their baby would be born healthy. Herman hired a nurse for Elsie while he was at work. Elsie supervised while Herman painted and wallpapered the bedroom they would use as a nursery. The day the baby furniture was delivered, Elsie went into labor.

Bradley Albert Pickett was born three weeks early. He was small but had a healthy set of lungs. Elsie held her son in her arms and whispered, "You will never want for a thing, my precious child."

Elsie kept that vow. Through the years, the Picketts never refused their son anything. They didn't use the word 'no' and gave in to his every want.

When Bradley was two-years-old, he grabbed another child's toy. The boy tried to retrieve his truck and Bradley hit him on the head with it causing a gaping wound that required stitches.

After other similar instances, the other mothers in the neighborhood wouldn't allow their children to play with Bradley fearing the injury his outburst could cause.

"Those women are jealous because Bradley is much cuter than their children," Elsie would say to Herman not realizing her toddler son was a bully.

The years passed by quickly. During Brad's early teen years, he spent hours in the principal's office for offenses ranging from cheating on a history test to causing a freshman girl to fall down a flight of stairs breaking her arm. Elsie and Herman were called to the school several times that year. Elsie complained that the principal unfairly picked on Bradley. "The other children are jealous of our son," she would say to Herman.

Brad's behavior improved in his junior year when he noticed his old classmate, Rebecca Wilson, had turned into a beauty.

Rebecca fought her attraction to the handsome, but conceited, Brad Pickett. He won her over and they became inseparable for the next two years.

Elsie noticed a change in Bradley. He seemed happier since Rebecca came into his life. She secretly hoped the two would marry someday and present Herman and her with a slew of beautiful grandchildren.

Her dreams were shattered when Bradley humiliated Rebecca at the dance. After hearing what happened that night, Elsie blamed her son for wrongdoing for the first time in his life.

"Son, I'm ashamed of you." Elsie's harsh words stunned Brad and he vowed to leave Oakwood Park as soon as he graduated and never to return to the crummy town again.

Chapter Six

Rebecca Snow arrived at the Oakwood Park Regional airport. She didn't understand why Carolina insisted she pick her up. It would be easy for her to rent a car at the airport. Rebecca didn't know why she was suddenly Carolina Bloom's best friend. They had never been particularly close in high school. Carolina tended to shy away from the girls and spend her time in the company of the popular boys.

***

That stupid bitch, thought Brad Pickett, *she expects me to be at her mercy. I should just come clean about my part in the insider trading scam. Sure, I'd be fired and would never work in finance again. I'd probably be fined and could be sentenced to prison. What is worse, being broke, jobless, and behind bars or putting up with Carolina Bloom's orders? I don't have a choice, but I'll get that woman out of my life if it's the last thing I do.*

Brad waited for Carolina to arrive. She'd told him to meet her at the airport and go along with her act. "Just keep your mouth shut and look at me like I'm the only woman in the world."

There were several people waiting for loved ones and business associates. Rebecca didn't notice the dark-haired man standing to the left of the crowd.

The reason he was here began to make sense to Brad. Carolina wanted Rebecca to see them together. Little did she know that Rebecca wouldn't give Brad the time of day. Her husband interrupted what should have been a happy reunion with the love of his life. He didn't know why he was hiding from Rebecca, maybe he was hoping Carolina would forget she ordered him to meet her at the airport.

The plane emptied out with the passengers greeting those who met them. Everyone was gone except Rebecca and the person standing behind her. Rebecca checked her phone to see if she had a message from Carolina saying she'd missed her plane or was detained in California for some reason.

She looked up and saw Carolina sauntering toward her with an exaggerated smile on her face. She batted her eyelashes and looked from Carolina to the man standing behind her.

"Bradley, darling, you came to meet me, what a delightful surprise. Rebecca, I won't need a ride from you after all."

Rebecca turned around and was surprised to see Brad standing there.

"Rebecca, dear, you remember Bradley Pickett from high school," Carolina said while throwing her arms around Brad's neck and kissing him.

Rebecca noticed the pained look on Brad's face. *What is Carolina trying to prove? Does she think I care if she and Brad have something going on?*

"As long as you have a ride to your hotel, I'll be on my way. It's good to see you again, Carolina," Rebecca said with more enthusiasm than she felt.

"Don't go, Rebecca," Brad said, "Let's all have a drink at the bar over there. We can talk about old times."

Carolina, still with her arm around Brad's shoulder gave him a pinch as a warning not to ad lib this meeting.

"I'm sorry, I don't have time today, I have an appointment I really must keep," Rebecca said turning to leave the terminal.

***

"I told you to keep your mouth shut. You will have to learn to follow orders, Bradley, or face prison time. Don't test me again, understood?"

"Yes, boss, I understand," Brad replied in a tone that sent a chill through Carolina's body.

***

Rebecca pulled her car into the garage. Andy greeted her at the door with a kiss.

"I didn't expect you so soon, darlin', did your friend miss her flight?"

"No, she was there and so was Brad Pickett. I get the feeling I was set up, but I don't know why.

Carolina flew into Brad's reluctant arms. Something is going on with those two and I'm not sure what it is, nor do I care. Brad suggested we have a drink in the airport bar and talk about old times. Carolina showed her displeasure by pinching him on the neck. I thought I imagined it until Brad winced in pain."

"Brad wants to get your attention. I don't blame him, you're quite the catch," Andy said while nuzzling his wife's neck.

Rebecca laughed, "speaking of catching, the club has their fish fry tonight, doesn't that sound better than leftover meatloaf?"

"I like your meatloaf, but let's go out. It's been a busy week; it will be nice to be waited on."

***

The Oakwood Park Country Club was famous in town for their Friday night fish fry. Rebecca and Andy were seated at a table for two by the window but not before stopping at other tables to greet their friends. The restaurant was busier than usual even for a Friday night.

"I don't want to be anti-social, but I'd rather sit quietly with you tonight, Andy."

"I feel the same way. I don't want to spend the evening listening to Cleve Jackson rehash his golf game, or Rob Gentry boasting about his latest romantic conquest."

"I can tell by the look on Mavis Jackson's face that Cleve is doing just that. I do feel sorry for Rob, he thinks he has something to prove because Charlotte left him for a younger man. His conquests are more wishful thinking than reality."

The couple sipped their extra dry martinis when Rebecca heard a commotion at the maître d' stand.

"Look, mister, I'm Carolina Bloom, I'm a famous movie star. I've been in better places than this and are always seated without a stupid membership card.

"Oh, there's my dear friend, Rebecca Snow, she knows me, let her know I'm here you imbecile."

"I wish I'd stayed home and heated up the meatloaf," said Rebecca, "this evening is not going the way I'd planned."

"George, it's okay, you can let Carolyn and her escort through. She's not a friend, dear or otherwise, but I do know her."

"I know who she is, Mrs. Snow, but I have orders to only allow members and guests to be seated."

"Put them on my tab, George. They will be our guests for tonight."

"Thank you, Mr. Snow, people like you make my job so much easier," replied George.

***

"Can you believe the nerve of that man, not letting me in? Hello, it's Andy, isn't it? Meet Bradley Pickett."

"Mr. Pickett and I have met; hello Brad."

"I'm sorry for barging in on you, I told Carolina this is a member only club, but she thinks because she is from Hollywood, she doesn't have to follow the rules."

"Oh, Brad, stop teasing me. Isn't he a treasure, Rebecca?"

Rebecca didn't answer the question and Brad looked extremely uncomfortable.

"Why are you two sitting at this tiny table? Let's have that stuck-up maître d' move us, so we can all sit together, wouldn't that be fun?" Carolina said in a louder than necessary voice.

"We were about to order dinner," said Andy while signaling for the waitress.

"Yes, said Rebecca, I'm afraid we have to eat and run. Our favorite television program is on tonight, we don't want to miss it."

"Television program? Rebecca, how do you bear living such a mundane life. I can't remember the last time I watched a television show."

"What do you mean, Carolina, the first thing you did when you checked into your hotel room was to turn on the television, I think you were watching some daytime soap opera. What was the name of that program? General Hospital? The way you were yelling at the characters, I thought you knew them."

"I turned it on to make certain it was working. These small towns try to get away with cheating their customers. The hotel promised television and I wanted to make certain they fulfilled their promise." Carolina scowled at Brad as he tried to hide a smirk.

After Andy ordered the fish fry for Rebecca and him, Carolina's mouth flew open.

"Rebecca, how do you expect to recapture your figure eating that horrible fried food. I'd be glad to share my diet secrets with you."

"Rebecca looks just fine to me," Brad said with a twinkle in his eye causing another scowl from Carolina.

It was unlike Rebecca to be vindictive, but Carolina was getting on her nerves, and she couldn't hold back. "Carolina, I'm one of the lucky ones, my metabolism is such that I have never had to resort to dieting."

Although Andy didn't appreciate Brad gawking at his wife, he had to snicker when Brad said, "I'd say Rebecca's figure hasn't changed since high school and look at her face, there isn't a wrinkle in sight."

Carolina tried to hide her fury as she sucked in her belly. It was true, she'd put on a few pounds in the last twenty years, but she still looked good. Milton gladly paid for her implants and didn't object when she had a little work done around her eyes and mouth.

"Let's find a seat at the bar and leave these folks in peace," said Brad as he dropped a fifty-dollar bill on the table. "This should cover her majesty's tab."

"That's not necessary, Brad," said Andy.

"Okay then, give it to the bartender, he'll deserve it after putting up with Carolina for the evening."

Chapter Seven

"Your instincts are correct, my dear. Those two are up to something," said Andy after Carolina and Brad were seated at the bar.

"I get the feeling Carolina is calling the shots and Brad isn't happy about her methods. If they are in a romantic relationship, it seems to be a strained one. Let's not talk about them, I'd rather talk about your day, you look tired."

"It's not so bad, the week seemed to go on forever, I'm looking forward to Kenzie's homecoming next month. Her smile brightens any difficult day, just like her mother's."

"How could I have forgotten to tell you? I heard from Mackenzie today. She is having a wonderful time in Europe. She sounded happy, I thought she might have met some handsome Frenchman who swept her off her feet, although she insists her only indulgence is in the pastries.

"I wish both our kids would decide to come back to Oakwood Park to live. Kenzie hinted she wouldn't mind living abroad and Alexander enjoys the fast pace in New York City."

"I'm not so sure about that. I ran into Jake Morgan this week. Jake said the last he'd spoken with Alex; he got the feeling he was tired of the city. He also asked about Kenzie, is something going on with those two?"

"I can't imagine there is anything between them. Kenzie had a huge crush on Jake when he and Alex were in high school. Jake was always kind to her, much more so than her brother. Of all Alex's friends, he was my favorite."

After finishing their dinner, Rebecca and Andy left their table waving to Carolina and Brad on their way out the door.

"Remember, we must rush home to watch our favorite television show."

"What is the name of that show?" asked Andy with a chuckle.

"I have no idea what's on tonight, I was afraid Carolina would ask me and I'd be forced to come up with something hoping to fool her."

"Let's have an after-dinner drink on the patio at home and count the stars. Remember when we used to do that with the kids? I guess I'm getting nostalgic thinking about our absent children."

Meanwhile, at the country club bar

"Bradley, you made a mess of that meeting. You were supposed to make Rebecca believe you were deeply in love with me. You are close to losing everything if you don't do better," Carolina said as she drained her second martini and signaling the bartender for another.

"No more for you, I'm taking you to the hotel. You have an appointment with Angus Carlson tomorrow morning, and you'll blame me if you oversleep."

Brad had his own room. He had no desire to share a bed with Carolina Bloom.

Carolina tried to argue with him saying with the time difference between California and the east it was still late afternoon. Between the travel and the drinks, she'd started at lunch, the oversized bed in her hotel room was more inviting than the little bottles in the mini bar.

"Brad stay with me, I don't want to sleep alone," she cried before closing her eyes and quickly drifted off to sleep.

Brad let himself out of Carolina's suite. He'd rented the room across the hall. It wasn't a suite, but it was large enough for him. He sat on the surprisingly comfortable sofa with a glass of scotch in his hand. He wondered how he'd gotten into this mess and remembered the night he spilled his gut to Carolina. He wondered why he'd had too much to drink that night. He was normally in control and hadn't had a hangover since his college days. Did Carolina put something in his drink that loosened his tongue? Had she really given a copy of his taped confession to a lawyer in California? Maybe he would leave the country, he'd change his identity. Did he really want to spend his life looking over his shoulder? His life wasn't worth anything with Carolina Bloom in it.

Brad's eyes began to close, and he fell asleep on the sofa with his drink in his hand. He dreamed of dancing with Rebecca, it was amazing how she'd kept her figure all these years. In his dream, he told Carolina she looked older than Rebecca. He woke up with a smile on his face.

***

In Angus Carlson's Office

"Carolina Bloom, I can't believe a movie star is sitting in my office. When you told me, you were returning to town I couldn't keep the news to myself. I told my assistant, Barb, and she blabbed the news all over town. I hope everyone is treating you well, it isn't often we have a famous person in our town."

"Angus, darling, thank you for your kind words. I have a wonderful proposition for you. What Oakwood Park needs is a local television show featuring the local folks with yours truly at the helm. It would be called *Carolina Bloom in the Morning.* Get it? Like the song…*Nothing could be Finer than to be in Carolina in the Morning.* Of course, we will include my full name to attract an audience."

Angus's first instinct was to tell Carolina that the station was doing fine showing reruns of old sitcoms. The viewers who watched the programs often bought the products advertised. The sponsors loved the lucrative time slot.

Angus was impressed with the confidence Carolina showed. He also admired her blonde hair and sparkling green eyes. Angus was partial to blondes although he married a brown-haired woman who was now totally gray. He'd have to convince his wife, Harriet, the true owner of the station.

"Carolina, do you have anything on tape that I can look at. You understand I can't take a chance like this without studying what you have in mind."

"No, Angus, I don't have anything to show you, however, if you get a cameraman in here, I can interview you."

Angus agreed and Carolina interviewed him. Angus thought she was a charming hostess. He only hoped he could get Harriet to agree.

***

"Angus, Carolina Bloom is a harlot, I can't have her running a show on my station with her sordid reputation. She married a man old enough to be her grandfather. I hope she doesn't set her sights on you."

"Harriet, my dearest love, there is no one in this world who compares to you. Besides, the scuttlebutt is that Carolina and a former Oakwood Park resident are an item. I will always be true to you, my darling."

"You'd better be if you want to keep your social standing in this town."

Angus had a soft spot for the young ladies. However, he prided himself on being very discreet.

His dalliances were either not known or not acknowledge by Harriet Carlson.

Harriet made Angus wait for her answer until she consulted with her psychic. The clairvoyant was enamored with movie stars and foresaw a long and successful run for *Carolina Bloom in the Morning.*

Chapter Eight

Carolina expected her show would start production the day after she signed the contract. Trying to save on costs and preserve the remaining money she had from Milton's estate, she fired her California agent and refused to hire a lawyer.

Her obstinance and her inflated self-worth almost put the kibosh on the deal. Angus Carlson was finally able to convince his promising star to let the staff do their jobs and when the show was a hit in the ratings, she would have more clout and could demand her ideas be implemented. Carolina was satisfied but anxious to do something other than lounge around the hotel pool all day.

She'd let Brad go back to his job but expected him to fly to town on the weekends to take her to restaurants frequented by Rebecca Snow.

"I meant to ask you, Carolina," said Brad, "how did you know Rebecca would be at the country club on that Friday evening?"

"Silly, I followed her to her house and waited for her to leave again. Because it was a Friday night, I guessed they'd be going out. I knew that snooty maître d would never let me in, so I made certain Rebecca saw me. I knew she would convince that dope to let us in. Rebecca has always been a pushover."

"You can't get away with following her in your car indefinitely. Someone is going to notice you watching her house."

"That's why I'm signing on with that stupid Community Playhouse. I'm planning to be Rebecca Snow's best friend. I'll know everything she does."

"I don't get it, Carolina, what did Rebecca ever do to you?"

"She didn't do anything, she just is."

"She just is what?"

"She just exists, everyone has always talked about perfect saint Rebecca. I was back in town a few years ago, and she was the talk of the town. She had the most wonderful husband and the best kids that were ever born. Even my mother sang her praises. I couldn't take it anymore. I had to get out of town. Rebecca is the one who encouraged me to go to California. I shouldn't have listened to her. Because of her, I married a control freak."

"You can't blame Rebecca for that, I doubt she ever met Harrington. You married the old codger because he was rich. It had nothing to do with Rebecca."

"The man stifled me, if I'd stayed in Oakwood Park, I'd never have met him, so it is Rebecca's fault."

"Has anyone ever said you are the most exasperating woman in the world?"

Carolina smiled, she knew if she waited long enough, Brad would forget about Rebecca and fall in love with her. She was determined to marry him and was willing to resort to more blackmail to get her way.

***

In the Snow kitchen

"Good morning beautiful, you made blueberry muffins, I could smell them in the bedroom," said Andy. "What's the occasion?"

"No occasion, I'm taking them to the playhouse this morning. Don't worry, I made enough for you, they are warming in the oven."

Rebecca's phone rang. It was Sandy Clark, the leader of the community theater.

"Rebecca, I hope I'm not calling too early, I wanted to talk with you before our meeting this morning. I was able to get the script for a stage play, *The Secrets of Willow Lake*. It's very risqué and nothing like we usually do. I think we can clean it up some, but I wanted to ask if you'd consider the female lead if we do it. I don't want the others to know unless you say yes."

"Sandy, I've read the reviews of that play. Are you sure we want to tackle something that dark? Our group is more into comedy and light mysteries."

"I know it's something different for us but maybe it's time we branch out."

"I can't promise, Sandy, but I'll read the script. I think the group should be told and let them decide."

***

"You look serious, Rebecca, was that bad news?" asked Andy.

"No, not bad news; Sandy has come across a script that is unlike anything we've ever done. It's a story about a woman who has secrets involving her love affairs and the murder of her husband. She wants me to play the lead. I don't think I want to do it. Am I being silly?"

"Not at all, I don't want you playing a part where you murder your husband. What if the character takes over and you slit my throat in your sleep?" Andy said with a laugh.

"That settles it, I'll sacrifice the part to save your life. It's too bad Carolina is doing her morning show; the part would be perfect for her."

"If that show ever gets on the air it will be a miracle, why don't you ask her. She can only say no."

"I'd rather not, the less I see Carolina Bloom the happier I am. She loves to flaunt her supposed love affair with Brad Pickett. For one thing, I don't believe Brad is a willing partner and for another, I don't care one way or the other."

In the Community Playhouse meeting room

Sandy Clark called the meeting to order. She noticed Barry Kemp in the back row and hoped he wasn't planning to audition for a part in their next production.

"It's nice to see so many faces today. It's nearing the end of summer and everyone is back from vacation. It's time to think of our autumn presentation.

"Rebecca and I have discussed an idea, she suggested I get your opinion. We have acquired the script of a play called *The Secrets of Willow Lake.* It is like nothing we have tried before. The language might be offensive to our audience, although we are at liberty to change the terminology if we choose."

Harvey Rutledge spoke up. "I know that story, it's hardly suitable for our best actress. No one would believe Rebecca Snow as the immoral Willow Lake."

"I agree with Mr. Rutledge," came a voice from the back of the room. "The part of Willow Lake was made for me." Carolina Bloom paraded up the aisle with her hips swinging.

"Carolina, I didn't realize you were in our group," said Sandy. "I didn't think you'd be interested in our amateur production with your talk show beginning soon."

"They are working out the details and I find I have time on my hands now that Bradley Pickett has returned to New York City. Of course, he will come back to Oakwood Park on the weekends. He can't stay away from me." She looked directly at Rebecca when she said it.

"We would be lucky to have a real movie star in one of our shows. I vote we do the play with Carolina Bloom as the star," said Elaine Becker.

The others chimed in with their opinions. Some of the more adventuresome agreed they needed to branch out, the more conservative members didn't like the idea of a suggestive presentation but were enamored with Carolina Bloom and voiced their approval.

Harvey Rutledge shook his head. He turned to Rebecca and whispered, "nothing good will come from this, Carolina is not to be trusted."

Chapter Nine

Carolina's talk show attracted more attention each day it was broadcast.

Harriet Carlson sat in her living room staring at the television set and seething. *Why did I let Angus talk me into hiring this Carolina person?*

She flirts with every male guest and insults the females. Just look at that skirt, her thighs are exposed. It's disgraceful. Look at her now, she's reminiscing with Mayor Reynolds about some stupid football game over twenty years ago. The mayor looks uncomfortable. I'm sure he wants to talk about funding highway expansion, and the little sexpot is reliving her cheerleader days.

Harriet dialed her husband's private phone. "Angus get that woman off the air. She is exposing herself right here in my living room."

"Harriet, *Carolina Bloom in the Morning* is a hit. The phones are ringing constantly. The folks in Oakwood Park and surrounding areas love Carolina's antics. Remember, dear, you signed a contract, and it will cost a pretty penny if we don't live up to our end."

"Shut up Angus, I'm wasting my time talking to you. You'd better not be involved with that woman outside of the studio."

It's not for lack of trying, Angus thought to himself, but said, "Dearest, you know you are the only woman I will ever love."

Mayor Adam Reynolds was squirming in his chair. Carolina Bloom was coming on to him in front of the television camera. He attempted to talk about highway expansion and she continually interrupted him to bring up long-forgotten stories of their high school days. He didn't remember much about Carolina back then. She was a beauty and still is, but he only had eyes for his future wife, Stephanie.

Just before they broke for a commercial, Carolina ran her toe on the inside of Adam's pant leg.

Adam's face turned red in anger. When he was certain they were off the air. He said, "Carolina if you try that again, I will walk off the set. The people of Oakwood Park want to hear about our overcrowded highways and not who won a football game twenty some years ago."

"Nobody wants to talk highways at this hour of the morning. I remember you in high school, Adam, you were a regular boy scout. What did Stephanie think of you driving Miss Rebecca home the night of prom? I'll bet you were a great comfort to her."

Adam was surprised to hear that Carolina knew he'd driven Rebecca home that night. Stephanie was the one to comfort her friend. Adam didn't want to further the discussion of that night, so he said nothing.

"I understand you are still married to little Stephanie Bower. You were always a good-looking guy, Adam, I'm sure you have escaped the monotony more than once."

They were back on camera before Adam could reply to her statement.

"The mayor insists on talking about a boring highway problem. You have the floor, Mr. Mayor."

Exactly one minute later, Carolina interrupted Adam saying they were out of time.

Adam walked off the set; the disgust showed in his face. "Angus, that appearance was a waste of time. You should have warned me that Ms. Bloom is uninterested in Oakwood Park."

"I'm sorry, Adam, Carolina is new to this type of show. She'll learn the ropes, and we'll have you back."

Adam didn't say it, but he knew he would never agree to another appearance on Carolina's show.

***

As time went on, *Carolina Bloom in the Morning* consisted of more gossip than information.

Her show was popular with young people and those who thrived on that type of program. The sponsors were happy because the show hadn't lost viewers who had been fans of sitcom reruns.

Harriet Carlson continued to complain to Angus and Angus continued to look longingly at Carolina when she was seated in her short skirts and low-cut blouses.

About half the calls the studio received were viewers praising the show. The other half were disgruntled folks who threatened to boycott the station if they didn't' stop showing filth.

***

Sandy Clark was sorry she'd considered doing the Willow Lake play. Carolina played the part perfectly. Willow Lake was a truly evil person and Sandy thought Carolina might have some of those traits.

Rebecca stayed behind the scenes. She helped with set decoration. She and Barry spent a half hour each day going over various scripts. He wasn't a bad actor; he was simply too nervous when there was a crowded audience.

"I wish you were starring in this play, Rebecca, everybody is happy on the set when you are in the starring role."

"I don't think it's me as much as the darkness of the play."

"Carolina doesn't help the mood any, does she?"

Everyone associated with the production of the play considered it a downer. All but Carolina were sorry they voted to perform it.

Sandy considered calling an end to it but there wouldn't be enough time to settle on another play and be ready in time for the fall presentation.

Carolina was either late for rehearsals or didn't make them at all. She was unpleasant to everyone except Harvey Rutledge. Although everyone called the old man Harvey, Carolina called him Mr. Rutledge.

Carolina managed to be on time for her television show. She liked being herself more than acting a part. She'd been so busy with the two projects; she hadn't pestered Brad to come to Oakwood Park every weekend.

Rebecca watched the show the first time and decided it wasn't for her. Adam Reynolds was one of the most honorable men she knew. She could see the discomfort on his face when he was on the show.

At the Playhouse

As usual, Carolina showed up at the playhouse twenty minutes late for rehearsal. The show was to go on in soon and timing still needed to be worked on.

Sandy Clark was certain the subject matter was the reason for the glitches. Again, she regretted attempting to do the play in the first place. Carolina was more of a challenge than Sandy had anticipated. She longed for the days when the regular crew joyfully practiced their lines, and everyone was interested in putting on their best performances.

"Carolina, you look pale, are you feeling all right?" Rebecca asked.

"No, I think I have the stomach flu and to top it off, I had a call from my mother this morning. I haven't spoken to her in years. She heard I was back in town and wanted me to know she was giving up the house and moving to a condo in Florida. She asked me to stop by and pick out anything I wanted to keep as a remembrance of my childhood.

"Why in heaven's name would I want anything to remind me of those horrible days with that horrible woman. I told her no and I'd see her in Hell. I know it's out of character for me, but I

70

feel bad that those are the last words I'll ever say to the woman who gave me life."

"Carolina, surely your mother knew you didn't intend to be insensitive. Perhaps you should visit her. It sounds like she was trying to reach out to you," said Rebecca.

"I'm not like you, Rebecca, I can't forgive and forget. You don't know what it was like growing up with a mother who never wanted you."

"No, I don't know what it was like and I wish your childhood were a happy one. There isn't anything you can do about that now except try to remember the good times. There must have been some of those."

Carolina smiled and sighed, "Mama taught me how to count to one hundred when she brushed my hair every night. I remember how gentle she was while brushing the tangles out. She told me her hair was just like mine when she was my age. I think I must look like my father in every other way, maybe that's why she resented me so much."

Rebecca's heart broke when picturing a young Carolina. She had no idea what it would be like to feel unloved by your mother.

"Would you like me to go with you to see your mother, I don't want to intrude but it might be easier to have a friend along."

"Are you my friend, Rebecca? I never had one before."

Rebecca wasn't sure what to think. Was Carolina being sincere? Was the change because she didn't feel well? Whatever the reason, Rebecca would be a friend if Carolina needed her.

Chapter Ten

Sandy Clark wasn't happy about Carolina leaving rehearsal so soon after her late arrival, but she could see the woman was distracted and knew rehearsing a pivotal scene in the play would require Carolina's full attention.

"Folks, there has been a change of plans. We'll meet tomorrow at one o'clock sharp," Sandy said looking directly at Carolina.

"I knew that girl was the wrong choice for our troop," said Harvey Rutledge. "Carolina Bloom was temperamental in high school, and she hasn't changed one bit. If you ask me, we should scrap the whole thing, what will happen on opening night if the prima donna decides not to show up."

"Harvey, we have so much invested in the show, we can't just give up. Look at the hours the crew has put in on set decoration alone. Rebecca is with Carolina now, maybe she can get her to cooperate with the rest of us."

On the way to the Bloom house

"Rebecca, this is a terrible mistake, turn the car around, I don't want to see Mama after all. I just want to go back to my hotel suite; I'm nauseated and too tired to deal with this."

"We're almost there, Carolina. You're probably just nervous, you'll feel better after you see your mother."

Rebecca turned to look at the woman slumped in the passenger seat. She did look miserable. *Is it more than nerves?* Rebecca wondered.

The house was in an older section of Oakwood Park. Rebecca guessed the gingerbread style home was built in the fifties. It was a perfect match for the woman Rebecca and her friends called 'the story lady' but not for a self-proclaimed movie star. A large real estate sign was placed in the front yard with the word 'sold' across it.

Carolina didn't flinch when she looked at the house. Although she was apprehensive about seeing her mother, she slowly opened the door of Rebecca's car.

"I can wait for you here, Carolina."

"Please come with me, I don't want to face the witch alone."

Ida Bloom stood at the front door waiting for her daughter to climb the few stairs to the porch.

"Hello, Carolina, I see you have taken to bleaching your hair. Too bad, it was your best feature."

"Mama, I'll have you know the finest stylists in Southern California have colored my hair with the best products on the market. They don't use household bleach."

"You're being impertinent, Carolina, I'm sure Rebecca doesn't speak to her mother that way."

Rebecca could tell Carolina was about to explode and did her best to change the subject.

"Ms. Bloom you have a beautiful home, you must hate to leave it."

"Rebecca, dear, I'm in my eighties and I can't take the harsh winters any longer. I'm looking forward to living in the Florida sunshine for the rest of my days. I can't say I'll miss this old place."

"Okay, Mama, what did you want me to take off your hands. I don't have all day."

"There's a box over in the corner with some things I thought you would like to have. There's an old grungy teddy bear in there. I can remember you carrying that thing around under your arm. I remember thinking you'd make a better mother than I did. You were always gentle with that bear.
"Carolina, I know I wasn't a good mother to you. It's no secret you were not planned for or even expected. I was too old to be a new mother. I should have given you away, but I couldn't do it. If you'd been adopted, you'd have had two parents to love you. I apologize for that."

"Mrs. Bloom, Carolina told me you taught her to count by brushing her hair every night. It's a nice memory for her."

"Is it, Carolina? I'm happy because I put that old hairbrush in the box too."

"When will you be leaving for Florida," asked Carolina?

"My flight leaves first thing in the morning. I'm only taking a few belongings. I have a furnished apartment on the beach. It's a place for the elderly, so I will be eating my dinner every night with all the other old crows living there."

"It will be nice for you to have company, Mrs. Bloom. Tell me, do you still read to children?"

"Oh no, I haven't done that in a few years. I don't read much anymore because my eyesight isn't good. I listen to audio books, so I'm up on all the latest works."

"Mama," Carolina said in a quiet voice, "would it be all right if I visited you in Florida?"

"Oh yes, I would like that very much. We'll sit in the sunshine by the ocean. I'll make sure I have a hat for you, we don't want the sun to ruin your beautiful hair."

Rebecca carried the box of treasures to her car while Carolina and her mother embraced for the first time in many years.

"Thank you for making me come, Rebecca, I feel so much better. I think Mama loves me a little after all."

***

It was the last time Carolina saw her mother alive. Ida Bloom died three weeks later as she sat on her lounge chair on the Florida beach looking at the ocean. She pictured her daughter sitting next to her with an oversized hat hiding her beautiful blonde hair from the sun.

If only Carolina had known her mama's last thought was of her daughter.

Chapter Eleven

Carolina struggled to get out of bed in the morning to do her television show. Continuing nausea made eating breakfast almost impossible. She did, however, manage to sip bottled pineapple juice from the studio refrigerator every morning. It helped to keep up her strength.

Partly because of her illness and partly because of her new friendship with Rebecca, Carolina's attitude changed. She tried cutting back on the gossip, but her audience expected it and tuned in to see what juicy tidbits they could learn that day.

The makeup artist worked diligently trying to hide the dark circles from the unforgiving television lighting. Carolina began to lose weight. The costume designer who volunteered at the playhouse was kept busy altering the outfits Carolina wore on camera. Rebecca quietly paid the woman for her services.

Rebecca thought of Carolina as an injured bird who needed care. Ida Bloom's death affected Carolina more than she thought possible and the sadness didn't help with her recovery.

"Carolina, you must see a doctor, a stomach virus doesn't last for weeks."

"I'll be fine, Rebecca, it's nice to have someone worry about me but I'll be better soon."

Carolina didn't get better. She barely made it through her television show and missed several rehearsals for the play. Sandy Clark knew *The Secrets of Willow Lake* would not be performed on the Playhouse stage.

"Harvey, I should have listened to you and Rebecca. This play was doomed from the beginning. I'm sorry our star is under the weather but sorrier for all the time and effort everyone wasted because of my ill-fated decision."

"Sandy, there might be a solution," said Harvey. "Mrs. Rutledge always tells me I'm a packrat and she's right. Because of it, I have a script that will please you. It comes from my college drama class. A humorous mystery called *Lilacs for Lyla*. I've looked over the sets from *The Secrets of Willow Lake* and, with a few adjustments, they will be useable. I've made copies of the script. I think you will find the storyline reflects the mood of today, although the play was written some sixty years ago."

Sandy was skeptical that starting from scratch on any new play was possible. She trusted Harvey and wanted to believe it could be done.

"Harvey, I have my doubts we can get our acts together, so to speak, by our fall deadline. Everyone, take the script home, read it over and come back tomorrow with your ideas of how we can pull this off. or if we want to."

"If Harvey thinks it will work," said Marsha Brill, "you have my approval today."

The others agreed with Marsha and began studying the script immediately.

"Just one thing," said Harvey, "Rebecca Snow must play the lead. It's a perfect part for her."

Rebecca agreed to do the play and as much as she enjoyed working with Barry and the others on set construction, she'd missed being on stage. Andy teased that she loved being a ham. It was true, Rebecca did like performing in front of an audience and she had always enjoyed visiting the world of make-believe.

On set at the television studio

"Where is Carolina, the show is about to begin in three minutes. Find her, Barry, she's probably in the makeup chair, it's taking longer than usual for the makeup girl to get rid of those dark circles and sallow skin color," shouted Angus Carlson. He knew Harriet would not be pleased if the show failed to begin on time. She'd commented only last night that Carolina looked emaciated. It was a harsh statement but not all that far from the truth.

"I'm here, Angus, don't be such a nag. Have I ever let you down?" said Carolina as she walked slowly across the floor passing out two steps from her chair.

"Someone call an ambulance," Angus cried nervously.

Carolina awoke and in an almost inaudible voice said, "No, I'm all right, I don't need an ambulance."

The program manager instructed the director to issue a notice that the station was experiencing technical difficulties. A rerun of a previous show aired in its place.

"Carolina, we can't allow this behavior to continue. I'm sorry you are ill, but I have a show to put on. Go home and get yourself together. We'll fill in with reruns of your shows for the rest of the week."

Harriet Carlson tuned her television set to *Carolina Bloom in the Morning*. Finding a rerun being shown, Harriet immediately called Angus demanding an explanation of what technical difficulties caused the removal of the live show.

Angus knew it was no use trying to hide the truth. He said Carolina was under the weather and he'd given her the rest of the week off.

"I want a live show by Monday, or we will go back to situation comedy reruns. It was a stupid idea to give that woman the job because of her looks. I told you not to hire her, but you had to do it your way." Harriet slammed the phone in Angus's ear.

Angus called Carolina to give her the bad news and that's when she said her friend Rebecca would fill in for her.

Now, I have to convince Rebecca to take over for me until I shake this flu.

Rebecca and Andy were finishing their dinner when Carolina called imploring Rebecca to cover for her by hosting *Carolina Bloom in the Morning*.

Chapter Twelve

After several weeks, Carolina's show was going well with Rebecca as hostess. The station received more rave reviews than when Carolina herself was in charge. Rebecca had a fresh and positive approach with her guests, and it brought out the best in them.

Rehearsals for *Lilacs for Lyla* moved along without incident and the play would be ready for its first showing within days of the scheduled opening. The *Secrets of Willow Lake* and the impending disaster was all but forgotten. The crew was upbeat and thrilled to have a mystery that was not only funny but heartwarming too.

Rebecca was tired after rehearsals and hosting the morning show, but delighted both were going well. She checked in on Carolina several times a week.

On a recent visit, Carolina asked, "Would you mind bringing me some pineapple juice? It's one of the few things that taste good to me. The studio ordered me several cases. I like the brand, but it isn't carried locally."

"I'll check with Mr. Carlson, I'm sure he won't mind if I take it since it was ordered for you."

"Don't ask the old grouch, he'll have to check with Harriet and if she knows it's for me, she won't allow it."

"Mrs. Carlson doesn't have a say in how her husband runs the station."

"Oh, yes she does, the old witch is the owner, Angus is merely an underling in the organization. He does what he's told."

Although the information was a surprise to Rebecca, it made sense. Harriet Carlson could be a difficult woman. She was a monetary contributor to the Community Playhouse and Sandy Clark answered to her upon occasion. Rebecca chuckled thinking about the reaction Harriet would have had to *The Secrets of Willow Lake*.

The following morning Rebecca visited Mr. Carlson's office.

"Mr. Carlson is in a meeting with the sponsor, Rebecca," said his assistant, Barb. "Is there something I can help you with?"

Rebecca replied she was there to ask Mr. Carlson's permission to take the bottles of pineapple juice to Carolina. She offered to reimburse the station for the cost.

"You don't need Mr. Carlson's permission; those juice bottles take up most of the room in the staff refrigerator. Carolina insisted we order them for her. No one else around here likes pineapple juice. We've been cramming our lunches and drinks in there. I promise it will be okay if you take the entire lot of them off our hands."

Rebecca had an hour between the ending of the morning show and the start of rehearsal for the play. It gave her time to stop by the hotel to deliver the juice to Carolina.

"I'll put them in the refrigerator for you," Rebecca said as she placed them one by one on the empty shelves. "I'll pour you a glass before I leave?"

After she left the suite, she passed a man in a dark suit walking toward Carolina's door. She assumed he worked for the hotel and had the feeling it wasn't a good sign that he had an angry look on his face.

Carolina was dozing off when she heard a loud knock on the door.

"Who is it?" she asked.

"It's Delbert Thorpe, Ms. Bloom. I'm here to discuss your bill."

Carolina opened the door. "Do you have to shout it to the world?" Carolina motioned for him to come in.

"Ms. Bloom, you are two weeks in arrears on your hotel bill. As financial director, I must insist you remit the entire amount, or I will have you removed from your suite."

"Mr. Thorpe, as I told you last week, I am waiting for my accountant to wire me money from abroad. I will pay my bill in full when it arrives. I'm afraid I've been under the weather and have let my obligations slide."

"You have my sympathy, Ms. Bloom, however, I must insist you pay within twenty-four hours or I will enlist our security guards to have you removed from the premises."

Delbert Thorpe turned to leave and winced when he heard the door slamming shut behind him.

All right, Bradley Pickett, it's time for you to pay up.

Bradley Pickett's mind was on only one thing when he answered his phone. He was preparing for his lunch date with the lovely Bianca. He'd met her the night before at a cocktail party and although he charmed her with his good looks and witty repartee, she refused his invitation to come home with him. There was nothing Brad liked better than a challenge.

"What do you want, Carolina, I'm busy."

"You're about to get busier Bradley, dear. You will go to your bank and withdraw ten thousand dollars cash. Bring the money to me before five o'clock tonight."

"Carolina are you crazy, I can't get my hands on that much money in such a short time. What do you need money for? Did you finally drain Milty's bank account?"

"If you must know, I need to pay my tab at the hotel. This antiquated town doesn't know how to treat a celebrity, I should charge them for my presence at their crummy hotel."

"So, they're going to throw you out on your privileged butt for not paying your bill." Brad tried to hide a chuckle.

"Shut up, Brad, get me the money or face the consequences." Carolina hung up before he could argue with her.

Stupid bitch, I've got to figure out a way to get her off my back. For now, I don't have a choice. I'll get the money for her, but this is the last time I'm caving into her demands.

At the Community Playhouse

Rebecca sat on a sofa backstage at the playhouse. She was waiting for her rehearsal scene to begin. It was nice to relax quietly, it gave her time to think. For the life of her, she couldn't understand Carolina's reluctance to see a doctor. She certainly didn't have a fear of plastic surgeons. It was obvious she'd had work done more than once. Had she been led to believe there was something seriously wrong with her? Something that would end her career.

"You are deep in thought, Rebecca, you look worried," said Barry Kemp when he stepped into the room.

"Hi, Barry, I was just thinking about Carolina, she's been sick for a long time and refuses to see a doctor."

"I don't think she's as sick as she pretends. She's laying it on to get sympathy. I must admit it has been happier around here, and at the studio, without her. No one likes her, including me."

"I know Carolina is difficult, Barry, but she's a person just like you and me. Her life wasn't easy, she didn't have the love of her parents as we did. I know you don't want her illness to continue."

"No, of course, I don't want that. Maybe she'll move back to California. That would be a good solution, will you mention it to her?"

It was time for Rebecca to check in for rehearsal. *Is Carolina disliked as much as Barry thinks? I hope it's not true but I'm afraid it is.*

Chapter Thirteen

"You certainly took your time getting here, Bradley. You'd better have the money with you or else," said Carolina when she opened the door to her suite.

Brad was speechless, he couldn't believe the change in the woman he hadn't seen for several weeks. Her hair looked stringy and had lost its luster; her face had a gaunt look he'd only seen on people forty years older than Carolina and close to death.

"Carolina, what the devil is wrong with you? You look terrible."

"Thanks, that is just what I needed to hear. Never mind, where's the money?"

"Don't worry, I brought it. All in cash, count it if you don't trust me."

"I don't trust you but I'm not going to count it."

Brad wondered if she was incapable of holding the bills long enough to count them.

"Here's what I want you to do, take this money to the financial office and give it to a dickhead named Delbert Thorpe. Tell him it will pay me through the end of the month and get a receipt for it. Come back here and we'll have a drink, I've got some of that good scotch you like."

"Carolina, do you think you should drink alcohol? It can't be good for you in your condition."

"What condition? I'm a little under the weather, that's all. If it makes you feel better, I'll have my pineapple juice."

***

Carolina was right, thought Brad, *Delbert Thorpe is a dickhead.* He didn't mind taking the money although he wasn't happy to hear Carolina would be staying through the month. Brad knew it was because he could rent the suite for an inflated price if a semi-permanent occupant moved out.

Brad walked back to the suite, he knocked and when Carolina didn't answer, he used the key she'd given him months ago.

Carolina was sound to sleep on the couch. Brad opened the liquor cabinet and poured himself a hefty glass of scotch.

He picked up a mirror he'd found on Carolina's dresser and put it under her nose. There was fog on the mirror indicating the woman was still alive.

Brad smiled to himself and began rifling through the drawers in Carolina's bedroom. If only he could find her copy of the flash drive, he would make an offer to buy the one she'd left with the attorney in California. Maybe a subtle threat would convince him to return the flash drive to its rightful owner.

After searching through every drawer in the suite, he reached under the bed and pulled out a small wooden box. Why hadn't he looked under the bed in the first place? Leave it to Carolina to pick the most obvious hiding place she could find.

Brad pried open the locked box with his car keys. The first thing he saw was a flash drive. He knew it was the one he was looking for. He spotted a piece of paper that looked tattered and colored with age. It was Carolina's birth certificate. The line for her father's name was blank. Brad felt a bit of sympathy for Carolina. He knew she'd never been close to her mother, and her father didn't think she was important enough for him to claim her as his own. He looked into the box again and saw a stamped sealed envelope addressed to:

> Bernard Winslow
> Winslow, Winslow, and Sloan
> 21005 Fourteenth Street
> Los Angeles, California 90071

Brad felt the envelope. *It's the other flash drive, Carolina never mailed it. I'm free.*

Brad swallowed his scotch and held his glass high. Thank you, Carolina, he said to the sleeping woman. Here's to your good health and mine. He couldn't keep the smile off his face as he stepped into the elevator and push the button for the lobby knowing he was leaving Oakwood Park and Carolina Bloom for the last time.

***

Carolina awoke without realizing she'd fallen asleep. She noticed an empty glass next to a bottle of scotch. Next to the bottle was a receipt for payment to cover her suite through the month. She was sorry Brad left. She'd hoped they could rekindle their romance. She knew he resented her since the first day she decided to blackmail him. Her plan had worked, he believed her attorney in California held evidence of his wrongdoing. She had neglected to send the flash drive to Bernard Winslow, but she would do it as soon as she began to feel better.

Carolina's nap made her feel groggy, she needed to splash water on her face. She walked into the bedroom on her way to the bathroom and let out a blood-curdling scream when she saw her wooden box opened on the bed. The flash drive and the envelope addressed to Bernard Winslow were gone.

"I could kill you, Brad Pickett, you low life creep. I hate you," Carolina cried aloud. She threw the box across the room; it broke open and a picture tucked between the lid and the lining fell to the floor. Carolina picked up the photograph, she recognized her mother in her younger days, standing next to her was a tall, handsome man. The resemblance to Carolina was uncanny. She knew instantly the man was her father.

Carolina couldn't put the photograph down. She walked to the refrigerator and poured herself a glass of pineapple juice. She was thirsty and drank the glass quickly. She then returned to the sofa and sat with the photo close to her chest. She closed her eyes and dreamed she was meeting her father for the first time.

Later that Evening

Maria, the maid, knocked on Carolina's door. When there was no answer, she used her pass-key to open the door.

"Housekeeping!" Maria called out. She entered the suite ready to pull down the covers of the bed. The maid normally placed a piece of chocolate on a doily for the guest's enjoyment. However, Carolina told her she couldn't stand the smell of the confection and to refrain from leaving it on her pillow.

"I'm sorry, Ms. Bloom, I don't mean to disturb you, I will come back later. Ms. Bloom are you ill?" she asked with concern. Maria walked closer to the sofa and saw a stream of dried blood coming from the corner of Carolina's mouth.

"Oh no, Ms. Bloom, I'll get help," Maria said although she knew it was too late. She called the operator who, in turn, called 911.

***

Detective Dan North arrived at the scene.

"Maria, did you touch anything in the suite?"

"No, sir, only the telephone on the table to call to report Ms. Bloom's death."

"How did you know she was dead?"

"I've seen death before, detective, my father was shot and killed while he drove me to school four years ago. A drunk driver ran over my brother when I walked him home from his baseball practice. I wish I could say Ms. Bloom was alive when I came into the room, but I knew it wasn't the case."

"I'm sorry for your losses, Maria, I won't keep you. Do you know why the bottle of alcohol was on the desk?"

"No, sir, I didn't notice it until now. I don't think Ms. Bloom had any of it. She was too sick to drink alcohol, the only thing she drank was pineapple juice and she drank a lot of that. She told me she was always thirsty, and it was the only thing that quenched her thirst."

"You may go, Maria, If I have any more questions, I'll let you know."

The coroner, Dr. Simon, arrived as Maria walked out of the room. He quickly examined the body.

"Does anyone know what this woman has ingested? My guess is poison. I'll need to get her to the lab as quickly as possible. Detective, until further notice, I recommend you treat this case as a homicide."

"Will do, Doc. Hamilton gather the juice bottles in the trash can and in the refrigerator. Also, the bottle of scotch and that glass. It's evidence so use extreme care. In fact, wrap up the toothpaste, toothbrush, shampoo anything edible in the suite. Check the cupboards for crackers, cookies, anything you can find although, by the looks of the body, I don't think the victim ate much."

"Dan, what can you tell me?" asked Greg Hoffman, a reporter for the Oakwood Park

Chronicle. "I heard the victim is Carolina Bloom. She's a local celebrity. Any leads? What's the cause of death?"

"Greg, you know better than to ask me questions I can't answer. The coroner is examining the body. I don't have any news for you at this time."

"I've got to get the story in for the morning paper, can you tell me if you suspect homicide?"

"Of course, I can't tell you that. Don't try putting words in my mouth."

"I won't but I have two sources who tell me the victim is Carolina Bloom. I'm going to run with it."

"I can't stop you, Greg, I wish you would wait until we have some answers before you *run with it.*"

Greg knew if the victim weren't Carolina Bloom, Detective North would tell him. His silence meant he could publish the information without fear of being sued for telling a falsehood.

Chapter Fourteen

After reading the headline about Carolina Bloom's death in the paper that Sunday morning, Rebecca felt physically ill.

"What kind of person lets a friend suffer without insisting she sees a doctor? I should have asked Dr. Whitcomb to see Carolina at the hotel. He'd have made the call and Carolina would be alive today."

"Rebecca, you don't know that" said Andy. "Carolina was a grown woman, if anyone is to blame, it's Carolina for being so stubborn. They suspect foul play. If that's the case and someone wanted her dead, you couldn't have done anything to change the outcome."

"I know Carolina could be difficult, but I can't think of why someone would want her dead. Barry Kemp mentioned that no one liked her at the television station. The poor woman didn't have any friends, except Brad Pickett. I'm not sure he was much of a friend, he seemed to resent being with her when he was in town."

At the Police Station

"Dan, Doc Simon is on line one."

"Thanks, Midge, I hope he has results for me, I have a few questions to ask certain people but not before we know the cause of death."

"My money is on unnatural causes, but you know what a cynic I am."

Dan smiled at his assistant as he picked up the receiver.

"Hello, Doc, North here, what have you got for me."

"Detective, it's as I suspected, the victim ingested minuscule amounts of rat poison over several months. According to the maid who checked in on her periodically during the day, the subject drank only pineapple juice and no other beverage or solid food for the last few weeks. The lab is testing the remaining juice bottles for traces of poison. This will be of interest; the entire case of fresh bottles was previously opened. I suspect someone compromised the pineapple juice before the victim consumed it."

"Thanks, Doc. I'll be anxious to hear what the lab finds. We seem to have a killer who was interested in torturing the victim with lingering effects of the poison. Did they enjoy watching the woman suffer?   Otherwise, why not kill her quickly?"

"I can't answer those questions, Detective, I've done my job, now it's up to you."

Dan called the lab. "How are you coming on those bottles of pineapple juice, Sammy?"

"The doc was right, Dan. Every bottle shows a speck of rat poison. Whoever did this wasn't looking for a quick death. We're waiting to hear from the FBI with the fingerprints found on the juice bottles and the scotch. Any luck finding out who was in the hotel suite enjoying a cocktail while the victim was dying?"

"We waited for verification of a crime being committed. I think we have enough to start asking questions."

At the hotel

"Mr. Thorpe, it's Peggy Simms, I'm sorry to disturb you on your day off. I'm calling about an incident that took place in the hotel last night."

"What kind of incident, it better be a good one, I'd planned to sleep in this morning."

"The guest in Suite D was found dead by the maid, late last night. The police are investigating. Detectives Dan North and his partner, Rob Granger are asking questions. I thought you should know."

"Suite D? That's Carolina Bloom's suite, I knew that woman was trouble. Don't answer any questions until I get there."

***

"Detective, Mr. Thorpe has instructed the staff not to answer your questions until he gets here."

"Who the devil is Mr. Thorpe?"

"Delbert Thorpe, he's the hotel's financial officer. He's in charge when the general manager is away."

"Why would you not answer my questions, Ms. Simms, do you have something to hide?"

"No, sir, I have nothing to hide, I didn't know Ms. Bloom. When she first arrived, she was in and out of the hotel often. She began her radio show, *Carolina Bloom in the Morning*. It wasn't long before Rebecca Snow took over for her. After that, she stayed in her suite. She didn't have many visitors. In fact, the only ones I remember are Rebecca Snow and a handsome gentleman who visited occasionally. Now that I think of it, he was here yesterday, he was leaving the hotel when I came back from my dinner break."

"As far as you know, he was the last person to see Carolina Bloom alive."

"I've said too much. Mr. Thorpe will have my head for not following his orders."

"I won't tell him, Peggy. You have been helpful. We will be doing a thorough search of the suite."

"Mr. Thorpe will be mad if I let you in the room."

"The room is a crime scene, Peggy. You don't have a choice and neither does Mr. Thorpe."

***

"Peggy, what is going on? Why are there policemen in Suite D? I told you not to do anything until I arrived. You disobeyed my instructions. I'll deal with you later."

"Officer, what is the meaning of this? What are your men doing in a private room of my hotel?"

"It's Detective North. I presume you are Mr. Thorpe. This suite is a crime scene. My men are looking for evidence in the death of Ms. Carolina Bloom.

"I see you signed a receipt for ten-thousand dollars in cash payment of rent on this suite until the end of the month. Who gave you the money, Mr. Thorpe?"

"I'm not answering any questions until my attorney is present."

"It's a simple question, Mr. Thorpe. I've checked with your bookkeeper and she only recorded an eight-thousand-dollar payment. Where is the rest of the money?

"Mr. Thorpe, how much do you know about the effects of rat poison on an individual?"

Delbert Thorpe's face turned beet red, his hands began to shake, and he reached out to the tabletop to steady himself.

"Okay, I did help myself to a lousy couple thousand dollars, but I didn't poison anyone. You can't pin this on me."

Suddenly, from the doorway of Suite D, a booming voice was heard saying, "Thorpe, you're fired, get your belongings and get out of my hotel.

Security will walk you to your office where you will hand over the money you stole."

Peggy Simms stood by the door trying to control the grin on her face.

"Detective, I'm Reginald Barkley, I'm general manager of this hotel. I was visiting my daughter in Pittsburgh and came back early this morning after being informed of our guest's death. What can I do to help you in your investigation?"

"Sir, it's unfortunate Ms. Bloom's death took place in your hotel. We believe she was systematically poisoned. The evidence indicates the source of the poisoning did not originate from the hotel or any of its facilities including the kitchen."

"That's a relief, after what I heard from Delbert Thorpe, I was beginning to suspect other members of the staff."

"I can assure you; everyone has been extremely cooperative beginning with Maria who found Ms. Bloom unresponsive to Peggy Simms who I'm certain Mr. Thorpe terrorized."

Dan received a call from the lab.

"We have the FBI results on the fingerprints found on both the juice bottles and the scotch bottle and glass.

"The juice bottles were apparently wiped clean, only fresh prints were found. They belong to Rebecca Snow. The scotch bottle prints were smudged but we were able to lift fresh ones from the glass. The only prints were of Bradley Pickett. I know Rebecca Snow; she took over for Ms. Bloom on her morning show. Bradley Pickett is a stockbroker from New York City. I hope it helps with your investigation."

"Thanks, Sammy, it gives me a place to start. I hope Mrs. Snow is in church this fine Sunday morning, she's going to need all the prayers she can get."

Chapter Fifteen

"Rebecca Snow?" asked Detective North when Rebecca opened her front door. He introduced himself and his partner, Detective Rob Granger, while they both showed their badges.

"Yes, Detectives, are you here because of Carolina Bloom's death? According to the newspaper article, you suspect she didn't die from natural causes."

Without responding to Rebecca, Dan asked if she is willing to answer questions.

"Yes, please come in. This is my husband, Andrew Snow. Andy these are Detectives North and Granger."

The detectives were all business as Rebecca led them to the living room.

"I can't think of any information I have that will be helpful."

"We'll be the judge of that, Mrs. Snow. How long did you know the victim, Carolina Bloom?"

"I knew her most of my life. We were both born in Oakwood Park and attended the same elementary and high schools. Carolina left town shortly after graduation. I hadn't heard from her until a few years later when she came back home for several months. She moved to California and only recently returned to Oakwood Park again."

"How well did you know her when you were in school together?"

"Not well, Carolina didn't seem interested in friendship. She was a beautiful girl, but she didn't have a happy childhood."

"Is it true you have taken over her job as hostess of her television show?"

"Yes, Carolina asked me to fill in for her while she was recuperating from an illness. I agreed because the station manager said he would cancel her show if she didn't come to work. Angus Carlson agreed to the change."

"What happens now, will the show carry your name?"

"Goodness, no one has thought that far ahead. I was a temporary hostess, not a permanent fixture. I have nothing to do with the future of the show."

"Mrs. Snow, what can you tell us about the bottles of pineapple juice in Ms. Bloom's hotel suite refrigerator?"

"Carolina preferred a special brand of pineapple juice the studio ordered for her. She asked me to bring her the extra bottles. It seemed to be the only thing she could keep down. Mr. Carlson's assistant gave me permission to remove them from the staff lounge. Carolina was the only person who drank pineapple juice."

"Are you aware rat poison was added to the juice and your fingerprints are the only ones found on the bottles?"

"What are you saying, Detective? You can't possibly think I tried to poison Carolina."

"Rebecca don't say another word," said Andy. "Detective, this interview is over until our attorney is present."

"Detective, I have nothing to hide but I agree with my husband."

"That is your right, Mrs. Snow. I'll expect you in my office tomorrow morning at nine o'clock."

***

"Ted Blake is on his way. He said not to panic, it's probably not as bad as it seems," said Andy.

"It's not Ted who is accused of murder. Andy, what am I going to do? My fingerprints are on those juice bottles. I couldn't be the only one to handle them, it's obvious they were wiped clean before I touched them."

***

Dan was glad he had time to investigate Rebecca Snow. She seemed like a nice enough lady but how many times had he heard victims exclaim how nice a proven criminal seemed.

Midge found an old high school yearbook in the research department archives.

Drama Club was the only activity listed under Caroline Bloom's name. Dan recognized Rebecca Wilson as the woman known as Rebecca Snow. It was obvious from the list of her activities she was an overachiever who'd also made the honor roll each year.

Looking through the yearbook, Dan noticed several photos of Rebecca with the same boy at a dance, at a football rally and other school-related activities. He wasn't surprised when he checked the photos of the senior class and recognized Bradley Pickett as the person with Rebecca Snow throughout the book.

"Rob," said Dan, "did you get an impression about the Snows marriage? Did Andy Snow seem angry?"

"He not only seemed angry, he was angry, but not at his wife. He was angry at us for suggesting Mrs. Snow is guilty of murder. I'm sorry, Dan, I don't buy it, I can't see that woman killing anyone."

***

Midge called from her desk. "Dan, Greg Hoffman from the Oakwood Park Chronicle is here, he wants to ask you about the Bloom case."

***

"Dan, you went to see Rebecca Snow today. Is she a suspect in the murder case?"

"How do you know that? Are you following me, Greg?"

"Sure, how else am I going sort this whodunit out? The people have a right to know and you are usually the most accommodating cop on the force."

"I have always told you everything I know when I have proof. I agree, the people have the right to know but reporters don't have the right to print a story without the facts. We have the supermarket tabloids for that purpose."

"I'm trying to avoid this story getting into the tabloids, Dan. Carolina Bloom was a celebrity, of sorts.   How much do you know about the relationship between Carolina and Rebecca Snow?"

"I never heard of either of them before the incident. What do you know?"

"Their rivalry goes back some twenty plus years. Carolina stole Rebecca's boyfriend the night of the senior prom. The boyfriend left Rebecca high and dry when he ran off with the willing Carolina. My mom was in their senior class and said Rebecca suffered from humiliation for the rest of the school year. It sounds like she finally got her revenge."

"Was the boyfriend's name Bradley Pickett?"

"Yes, how did you know that? I guess you have done your research after all. What can I tell my readers?"

"Look, Greg, I can't tell you anything, we will talk to Mrs. Snow tomorrow along with the staff of the television show and the folks from the playhouse. You'll be the first to know if we solve this case."

Greg left the police station. His next stop would be his mother's house. His mother was always good for the latest gossip in town. He was sure he could coax her to remember her high school days and the Rebecca, Brad and Carolina triangle.

***

"Rob, is it possible to hold a grudge for over twenty years?"

"Sure, I'd still like to punch Joe Barnes in the nose for stealing my girl in eighth grade. Do you think Mrs. Snow still resented the Bloom woman? Killing an old rival seems extreme, but I suppose murders have taken place for less reason."

***

Dan poked his head out the door. "Midge, see if you can find an address and phone number for Bradley Pickett."

"I'm on it, sir," Midge replied.

Chapter Sixteen

"Rebecca," said Ted Blake, "I know you are upset about being questioned by the police. You and I know you are innocent of any wrongdoing and the evidence is flimsy. I want you to tell me everything you can remember about your encounters with Carolina Bloom since her recent arrival in Oakwood Park."

Rebecca told the attorney everything she could remember. She talked about how strange it seemed that Carolina often appeared where Rebecca was, "I thought I imagined she was following me. If she was, it stopped when she began to feel ill."

"I don't like to mention this, but I've heard Brad Pickett has been seen around town with Carolina. Did that bother you?"

"Oh, Ted, why does everyone in this town think I'm still smarting over that stupid prom and the fact that Brad left me there while he went off with Carolina. I admit, I was humiliated that night, but I got over it. You are looking at my consolation prize." Rebecca said smiling at Andy.

"Yes, you did end up with a good guy. My little sister had a crush on Brad, I thought he was a jerk."

"You were right, he was a jerk then and a jerk now."

"Have you seen much of him since he's been back in town?"

"Only when he was with Carolina. She flaunted him like a trophy. He always seemed uncomfortable being with her. Oh, he came to our house one time. I was on my way to a meeting when he showed up. I hadn't seen him in years, but I'd heard he was in town. Luckily, Andy showed up, and he left willingly."

"Were you frightened of him?"

"No, he wasn't frightening, I didn't have the time or the interest in a mundane chat with an old flame."

"Did anyone see him arrive?"

"I don't know, why do you ask, Ted? You don't think there was something going on between Brad and me."

"I don't, I'm anticipating questions you might be asked. The police don't always play nice when they have a murder to solve."

Rebecca fought back the tears. Andy told the attorney he knew his wife and trusted her. "Ted, the police can't be thinking Rebecca did this horrible thing. Anyone who knows her knows she isn't capable of murder."

"The detectives don't know Rebecca, Andy. Dan North and Rob Granger transferred from a department up north."

"Half the folks in town will gladly be character witnesses."

"Andy, the police have questions for Rebecca. No one is talking about a murder trial."

Ted left saying he'd be back in the morning to drive them both to the police station. He didn't trust Andy to keep his mind on the road.

***

Greg's mother, Carol Hoffman, greeted her son at the door.

"Greg, what a nice surprise; what brings you by?"

"Mom, I want you to tell me everything you know about Rebecca Wilson Snow."

"Do they think she killed Carolina? Oh, my goodness, what a story that would be. You know their rivalry goes back to their senior year in high school when Carolina stole Rebecca's boyfriend right out from under her nose."

"Yes, Mom, how much do you know about their relationship now?"

"I can only guess. You know Carolina hosted this horrible television show in the morning. It was shameful with talk of sex and infidelity. That was before they pulled her off the air because of some strange illness and put Rebecca in her place. It was a whole different show then; Rebecca didn't have smut on it.

"Did you know, the Community Playhouse was going to put on a play starring Carolina? I heard Rebecca was so mad she refused to play second fiddle to the likes of Carolina Bloom. Eventually, they changed their minds and told Carolina they weren't doing the play after all. Guess who's the star of the substitution?"

"Mom, I understand Carolina was too sick to do her show or act in a play. Are you sure it wasn't because of her illness they decided not to do the play?"

"That's what Mary Lou Franklin told me. Mary Lou is the agent who sold Elsie Pickett's house. She said Bradley told her to handle the sale and get what she could for the place. He had no intention of coming back to Oakwood Park. However, when Carolina showed up in town, Bradley was waiting for her at the airport. There was something going on with those two. Carolina pranced around town on Brad's arm like she was flaunting their romance. If you ask me, Rebecca did better with her marriage to Andy Snow. Now, thanks to Brad Pickett, it will be curtains for that marriage. Of course, Rebecca could spend the rest of her days in jail."

Greg left his mother's house thinking *the woman needs a hobby, she has too much time on her hands.* He couldn't use any of her gossip although he wondered why Brad Pickett would pick up with Carolina again.

***

"Dad," cried Alexander Snow over the phone. "I read about Carolina Bloom's death online. They say mom is a person of interest. Dad, I'm coming home."

"Alex, they are talking to your mother, she is one of the few people who knew Carolina. I'm sure they can't charge her with a crime she didn't do."

"Dad, I'm booking a flight as we speak. You stay with Mom; I'll rent a car or catch a ride to your house. Have you spoken with Ted Blake?"

"Yes, he came over today and will be with your mom tomorrow when the police question her again."

"Good, looks like I'll be in around seven. I'll see you then. Give Mom a hug."

***

"Alex, it's Jake.   Has your mother called you?"

"No, I called Dad when I read Mom is a person of interest in a suspicious death. I'm on my way to the airport."

"I'll pick you up, what time does your flight get in?"

Alex could count on Jake to be there for him and his family. Jake had been his best friend for as long as he remembered. No matter the distance between them, they were still best friends.

Chapter Seventeen

Despite Rebecca's delight in seeing Alex at her door, she said he shouldn't have traveled all this way.

"Your job is too important, you are doing good work and I don't need you to hold my hand, although I am happy, you're here."

"I couldn't let you and Dad go through this without being home. I know Ted will represent you well. He's a good man and a good lawyer."

"I'm not worried," Rebecca replied. "That's a fib, Alex, I've never been so frightened before. A woman was poisoned, and my fingerprints are on the bottles containing the poison."

"You have every right to be frightened, you will not like this, I called Kenzie, she's coming home."

"No, Andy, call her, tell her I'm fine. She's having such a wonderful time overseas. I've disrupted both our children's lives."

"Mom, we want to be with you, so stop worrying about us. You don't mind if Jake and I grab a beer?"

"Where are my manners, let me get beers for you. How about a nice ham sandwich, you must be starving?"

"Maybe later, I want you to tell me anything you can think of. Why was Carolina Bloom in Oakwood Park? Did Brad Pickett follow her here, or did Carolina follow him?"

"Alex, that's enough, your mother has been answering questions all day," Andy said as he handed his wife a martini with a twist.

Rebecca smiled. "Just what the doctor ordered," she said as she sipped the drink. "Andy, Alex has come all this way, the least I can do is tell him why the police suspect me of cold-blooded murder."

"No, Dad's right; you've been through enough for one day. Relax and drink your drink. I have some news of my own."

"You've met someone!"

"No, nothing like that. I've been thinking of moving back to Oakwood Park. I shouldn't have left in the first place. The law office takes up four floors in the building. I'm on the 22nd floor and I've never met most occupants of the 26th floor. They are all vice-presidents and officers and such.

"My good intentions of being a lawyer to help those in need quickly faded as I was caught up in my quest to reach the 26th floor. My cases involved researching legitimate allegations against corporations and disproving the claims.

"When Dad called me today, I knew Oakwood Park is where I want to be, not only to be with you while the police investigate Carolina Bloom's death but for the foreseeable future."

"Alex, that would make me so happy, however, I want you to take time to think about your decision. I'm sure this thing will be cleared up in a day or two. Several people disliked Carolina; I have to figure out who disliked her enough to kill her."

"That's enough talk about murder," said Andy, "let's relax with our drinks; I'll get you boys those beers unless you want something stronger."

"Thanks, Mr. Snow," said Jake, "a beer sounds great. Alex, when did you say Kenzie will arrive in town?"

"Sometime tomorrow, she figured around eleven o'clock. She'll call when she knows the time. Why do you ask? Don't tell me you want to see the little pest?"

"It will be good to see her, she wasn't a pest, you were mean to her if I remember. I tried to be her friend. Anyway, I thought I could pick her up at the airport since you folks will be busy in the morning."

"Gee, that's nice of you, Jake. Mom, is it okay if I move that photo of Kenzie closer to Jake so he doesn't have to strain his neck to stare at it?" Alex laughed.

"You caught me, okay, I admit, I'm anxious to see the little twerp all grown up. She really turned into a beauty."

Rebecca and Andy smiled; they were both thinking how nice it would be to have Jake Morgan in the family.

The foursome shared a nice evening, unfortunately, by bedtime, the effects of the martinis had worn off and Rebecca and Andy slept fitfully until morning.

***

"Hi, Alex, how's Mom doing?" Kenzie asked when she called from the terminal at JFK.

"She's being questioned by the detectives. Ted Blake is in with her. Dad's nervously pacing the floor. When do you get to Oakwood Park?"

"The plane lands at eleven forty-five. They are boarding now, so I'd better go. Tell Mom and Dad I love them and don't worry about me, I'll take a cab to the house."

"No, don't do that. Jake Morgan will meet you at the airport. You remember Jake, don't you?" Alex asked with a knowing laugh.

"Do I remember dreamy Jake? Yes, is he still as gorgeous as he was when I was a kid?"

"No, he's pretty ugly, you'll recognize him by the warts on his face."

"Oh, shut up, Alexander. You'd better treat your little sister nice; I know all your secrets."

Alex called Jake to let him know Kenzie's arrival time. "She wanted to know if you are still gorgeous and I told her 'no, you are still as ugly as ever.'"

"Good, then she'll be delightfully surprised when she sees I'm still gorgeous. We'll see you at your house. Hope everything is going well with your Mom."

"We'll find out soon. See you later, pal. No stopping on the way at some sleazy bar with my kid sister."

"Don't worry, we'll come straight from the motel," Jake laughed.

***

"Mrs. Snow, Mr. Blake, thank you for coming in this morning," said Detective North.

Rebecca glanced on his desk and noticed a copy of her high school yearbook. She knew he'd probably left it where she could see it to see what her reaction would be.

"Mrs. Snow, when did you rekindle your romance with Bradley Pickett?"

"Detective, you know that is not a proper question," said Ted Blake.

"I'll be happy to answer, Ted. I do not have a relationship with Brad Pickett. He was my boyfriend in high school and, as you know, he left me alone at our senior prom while he went off with Carolina Bloom. Our relationship ended that night. After graduation, I hadn't laid eyes on him until a few months ago when he arrived at my doorstep uninvited. I'd have forgotten about the prom episode long ago if you and others didn't remind me of it constantly."

"Did you hate Carolina Bloom for helping humiliate you that night?"

"I have never hated anyone in my life. I tried to be a friend to Carolina. I'd learned her childhood was not a happy one, and I sympathized with her. The reason my fingerprints were on those juice bottles was that she'd asked me to bring them to her.

I did as she requested and placed them in the refrigerator in the kitchen of her hotel suite."

Dan held the yearbook in his hand. "There are several photographs in here of you and Bradley Pickett. A love like that doesn't end after one little tiff."

Rebecca felt Ted's hand on her arm. He knew he was telling her to calm down and not take the bait.

"Detective North, it was a high school romance; I was too young to know about love. I didn't find it until I met Andrew Snow."

"You had to be jealous of Carolina Bloom for running off with your boyfriend on the most important night of your young life."

"No, I wasn't jealous, in fact, I didn't know it was Carolina until recently. It seems the entire town knew the whole story, but I was in the dark."

"Who did you think he was with?"

"I know I was naïve, I thought he'd gone to some bar on the outskirts of town to drink beer with his buddies. I figured he'd picked up some floozy. After Carolina came to town, someone mentioned she'd been the one Brad was with that night."

"What was your reaction to that bit of information?"

"I was surprised, but it was a long time ago and it doesn't matter who he was with that night."

"How long did it take to get over the humiliation?" Dan asked.

"Not long at all. My older sisters took me to New York City to get my mind off the dance. We were interviewed outside the Today show where I told my story and could laugh about it. By the time I got back to Oakwood Park, most of my friends had seen a tape of the show and praised me for my courage. I'm not sure I was courageous; it was my sisters who made me realize my world hadn't ended."

"Your world didn't end but Carolina Bloom's world did. That's it for now, Mrs. Snow. I'll let you know if we have anything further."

***

Rebecca and Ted walked out of the detective's office and were greeted by Andy and Alex.

"She did beautifully, I wish all my clients were as persuasive as Rebecca, I don't think Detective North will bother you again."

"Do you really think it's over, Ted? Someone caused Carolina's death and I want to find out who. I owe the woman that much."

"Rebecca, what do you owe Carolina Bloom?" Andy cried. "She embarrassed you by flaunting your old boyfriend in your face. She wasn't a kind person."

"Andy, look what I have, a fabulous husband, wonderful kids, and great childhood memories. Carolina had none of that. She deserves to have someone on her side even after her death.

"Now, let's get home and wait for our daughter's arrival. I can't wait to see her."

Chapter Eighteen

Barbara Tinsdale, Mr. Carlson's assistant, sat nervously in the waiting area of the police station. Detective North had summoned her for questioning.

Barb is a slightly built woman who has worked for the Carlsons for twenty of her fifty-three years. Although she is small in stature, she portrays herself as a no-nonsense woman who frightens the staff members into staying in line. Although only a few years her junior, Barry Kemp is like the son Barb never had.

Barb knows the station operation better than Mr. Carlson. When Carolina Bloom arrived in town several months ago, Barb advised her boss to not be persuaded by Carolina's looks.

"That woman is trouble Angus, no good can come from hiring her."

"Nonsense, Barb," Angus replied, "Carolina will bring a much-needed boost to our morning ratings, just you wait and see."

Barb wasn't easily intimidated but waiting to be questioned by the police was a long way from her comfort zone. The scuttlebutt around the television station suggested poison killed Carolina. Did the police consider her a suspect?

Barb had her share of run-ins with Carolina often during the time she was hosting her show. The woman was impossible to work with, she was rude and demanding. That stupid pineapple juice was a prime example. It had to be a certain brand purchased from a certain store and kept at a certain temperature. She lost track of the times Queen Carolina demanded Barb deliver a bottle of her pineapple juice to her dressing room.

The first time she brought it, she'd neglected to bring a straw. "Carolina Bloom does not drink from a bottle," she bellowed and threw the bottle against the wall. "Bring me another with a straw this time, you idiot." Barb did as she'd asked and resisted the urge to spit in the second bottle before she delivered it.

***

"Ms. Tinsdale, thank you for coming, please follow me to my office, my partner and I have some questions to ask you."

"I'm sorry, Detective, I've never been inside a police station before and never been questioned by the police. Do I need to hire a lawyer?"

"It's your choice, Ms. Tinsdale, however, we are gathering information, this isn't an inquisition. If you feel intimidated, we will end the questions until your attorney is present."

Barb felt more relaxed. The detective wasn't as scary as she'd pictured. His partner, Detective Granger, had an angelic face and that, too, was reassuring.

"Ms. Tinsdale, being Mr. Carlson's assistant gives you the advantage of knowing the other staff members. Midge, the lady you met earlier is the captain's assistant. She knows most of us better than we know ourselves. It's Midge we go to when we are having trouble with a case or in our personal lives. Midge always has sage advice for us. I'm sure the staff at the television station feels the same way about you."

A smile spread across Barb's face. "Yes, sometimes I feel like a mother hen. Your Midge and I have a lot in common."

"Barb, how did your chicks feel about Carolina Bloom?"

"Oh my, Queen Carolina was disliked by everyone at the station. I didn't care much for her myself. I shouldn't say everyone, between you and me, I believe Angus Carlson had a crush on her. Not that I blame him, Harriet Carlson is a cold woman. She owns the station, you know. Oh goodness, how that woman carried on when Carolina's show aired. After Rebecca Snow took over, Mrs. Carlson calmed down. Rebecca is a lovely person and the polar opposite of Carolina Bloom."

"Ms. Tinsdale, who ordered the pineapple juice Ms. Bloom requested?"

"Oh, that pineapple juice. She was so fussy about her pineapple juice. I ordered it as she demanded. Mr. Carlson gave his approval. If she'd been able to work before that supposed illness took effect, I'm certain her demands would have grown."

"You don't believe she was ill?"

"No, who has the flu for months at a time. She thought she could get away with faking an illness and get paid for not working. Well, Mrs. Carlson put a stop to that after the very first week. Everyone was happy when Rebecca took over the show."

"Back to the juice, was it delivered to the station?"

"Yes, it came by the case. I ordered enough to last six months. I'd fill the refrigerator with half a case at a time. It took up most of the room in the small refrigerator and the rest of the crew had to squeeze their lunch bags in around them. I was glad when Rebecca got rid of them."

"Did you know the juice bottles contained rat poison?"

Barb's mouth dropped. "How can that be, the manufacturer is reputable. I've not heard of the juice being recalled."

"We believe the poison was placed in the bottles after it arrived at the station."

"Are you accusing me of murder?" Barb said fearing she had said too much already.

"I'm not accusing you of anything, Ms. Tinsdale, however, someone at your station might have tampered with those juice bottles. Do you have any idea who it could be?"

"No, the bottles were in the refrigerator or in the closet in the staff lounge. The closet isn't locked, everyone has access to it." Suddenly, Barb remembered Brad Pickett waiting for Carolina to finish her show.

"You've thought of something or someone."

"Yes, I didn't much care for Carolina's boyfriend, but I don't want to accuse him of murder."

"Are you talking about Brad Pickett?"

"Yes, while Carolina was doing her show, he would wait for her in the staff lounge. It was early in the morning and breaks weren't scheduled until later. He'd switch the television from our station to the business news channel. I asked him not to do it, but he did it anyway. He was alone in that room for over an hour almost every day for months.

"Sometimes he'd come to my desk and talk to me during the commercials. He was arrogant and self-centered. Anytime I mentioned Carolina's name he had a look of disgust on his face and changed the subject. I remember wondering what she had on the guy, it was obvious he wasn't seeing her because he had feelings for her."

"Barb, you have been helpful, there is one more thing. Is there a reason there weren't any fingerprints left on the bottles?"

"That's easy, I wore gloves when I took them out of the cases and wiped off the accumulation of dust before I put them in the refrigerator. If Carolina saw a speck of dust on the bottle, she would know I'd ordered them months before. The bottles in the refrigerator were the last. I didn't reorder because I hoped we'd seen the last of Carolina. Oh, dear, Detective, I didn't mean it the way it sounded."

The detectives thanked Barb for her cooperation and asked Midge to escort her to the lobby.

"That lets Rebecca Snow off the hook. Whoever poisoned those bottles, was fortunate Carolina was particular about when her pineapple juice was purchased. I'm glad I never met the woman, she sounds like a piece of work," said Rob Granger.

"Let's get Bradley Pickett in here right away, I don't want the guy disappearing on us."

Chapter Nineteen

Mackenzie Snow checked her messages after the airplane landed. Alex texted her to let her know their mother wasn't being charged and most likely wouldn't be in the pokey when she got home.

Kenzie never doubted her mother for a minute but was glad the ordeal had ended. She was glad to be home. Traveling across Europe had lost its charm when a handsome Frenchman offered to make her his mistress. She thought no one could make another person feel tainted, but Adrien Bisset did just that.

Rebecca was supportive when Kenzie called saying how happy she was living in Europe. Kenzie could hear the sadness in her mother's voice. She didn't mention the reason for her happiness and now that Adrien was out of her life, she longed to be home again. When Alex called about their mom being in trouble, she couldn't wait to book her flight to the United States and home.

Her heart skipped a beat as she got closer to the waiting area knowing she would see Jake Morgan again. At thirteen she was hopelessly in love with Alex's best friend. She shuddered when she remembered how obvious she'd been in her adoration.

Kenzie spotted Jake immediately, she recognized his beautiful smile. He was better looking than he'd been as an eighteen-year-old.

"Kenzie, you look terrific. I'm sorry you had to come home under these circumstances. Alex said your mother isn't under suspicion. I know your family will be happy to have you back for a little while."

"Alex texted me that the police let Mom go. They don't know my mother, or they wouldn't have questioned her in the first place. I'm not here for a visit, wait until you see the luggage I brought. It's everything I own in the world; I hope Mom didn't turn my room into a man cave for Dad."

"Your dad doesn't seem to be the man cave type. Your house will be a busy place, sounds like Alex is coming back to Oakwood Park himself."

"What happened to Delia? I thought those two would conquer the world together?"

"Alex came to his senses. Delia left him for some old guy at the firm. He seemed more relieved than heartbroken. Speaking of heartbroken, I hope that's not the reason for your return."

"No, not heartbreak just disappointment. I was gullible and fell for a line of baloney. I should have known better, but it sounded nicer in French."

"Were you in love with the guy?" Jake asked

"In love? Heavens no, I said I was gullible not stupid. Let's not talk about my non-existent love life. What about you Jake? I know you aren't married, or Alex would have told me. He likes to tease me about my embarrassing crush."

"I have nobody, my mom tells me I'd better find a girl soon to give her grandchildren or she'll be too old to enjoy them."

The baggage carousel turned interrupting their conversation.

On the ride from the airport, Kenzie was quietly staring out the window.

"Everything looks different, it feels like I've been gone for twenty years. Funny, it looks different, but it feels like home."

***

Jake pulled the car in front of the house. Rebecca, Andy, and Alex all ran to greet her. Rebecca and Kenzie didn't fight the tears. Andy was choked up and Alex hurried to get the suitcases from Jake's car trying to keep from blubbering himself.

***

After settling into her old room, Kenzie and Rebecca joined the men at the kitchen table where Andy had prepared a large plate of cold cuts and cheeses along with oversized Kaiser rolls from Alex and Kenzie's favorite bakery.

"Dad, as much as I love French pastry, I've been craving these rolls," said Kenzie. "With all, you and mom have been through I can't believe you made a special trip to Iola's Bakery."

Andy smiled, he was happy to have his family together and Rebecca's ordeal behind her.

***

"Rebecca, I'm glad you picked up," said Angus Carlson when he called. "Does that mean you are no longer a suspect in Carolina's murder?"

"Angus, I don't believe I was a suspect, the police wanted to ask me a few questions. Thank you for your concern," Rebecca said knowing he called because he wanted something.

"Good! We will broadcast day after tomorrow. We'll do the show that we'd planned for today."

"Angus, do you think that's appropriate? How can you present *Carolina Bloom in the Morning* when the star of the show is dead?"

call it *The Morning Show with Rebecca Snow.*"

"That's a terrible idea. I was filling in for Carolina, I'm not qualified to host a television show permanently."

"Rebecca, you are a natural. Carolina had minimal success for the short time she hosted. Once you took over, the popularity, and the ratings soared. Don't underestimate your talent, our audience loves you."

"Angus, I will think about it, my children are here visiting, and I don't want to miss any time with them."

"You will be home by eleven o'clock every day. You know how young people like to sleep in, you won't miss any time with them."

"I'll get back to you, Angus."

***

"What was that about, Mom, you look confused."

"I am, Alex. I have something to discuss with you. Where did Kenzie run off to?"

"She walked Jake to his car. I'd say he stopped thinking of her as a little girl."

"I, for one, think it's terrific. I always liked Jake Morgan."

"Me too, and despite my protests to the contrary, I always liked my little sister too."

***

The Snows gathered around Rebecca hoping the phone call wasn't Detective North requesting another meeting. Rebecca told them Angus's plan and wanted to know what they thought.

"Mom, that's terrific; my mother, the television star," said Kenzie.

"Mom, I'm happy for you but I want to go over the contract before you commit," said Alex.

"You are wonderful in front of the camera, dear. Is it something you'd like to do?" Andy asked with pride.

Rebecca admitted she enjoyed the challenge of doing the show. She decided she would try it; however, she didn't want her name in the title.

Angus agreed to a three-month trial insisting she begin the next day.

***

The first ten minutes of the show were difficult. Reginald Barkley, the Oakwood Park Hotel owner, authorized Rebecca to look through Carolina's belongings for photos and mementos for the broadcast. She and Barb Tinsdale hit the jackpot when they found boxes of photos and tapes from Carolina's time in California.

The interviews of those who knew Carolina Bloom didn't go as smoothly. She'd burned too many bridges with her caustic words and bad behavior. Brad Pickett refused to be a part of the show.

Chapter Twenty

Detective North requested Brad's presence in his office.

"I have nothing to tell you, Detective. Carolina and I had a casual friendship, nothing more."

"Pickett, either you come on your own accord or I will have you arrested on suspicion of murder. Either way, you will be questioned."

***

Barb Tinsdale called Brad's cellphone while he was driving to Oakwood Park. He could barely control his temper when she asked him to comment on his friendship with Carolina.

"Look, lady, I have nothing to say about that woman. I went along with her scheme to make Rebecca Snow jealous only to get closer to Rebecca. If I told you what I really thought of Carolina, your entire show would be censored."

Brad didn't intend to say as much as he did. His euphoria at finding and destroying the incriminating flash drives was overshadowed by the fear he would be accused of murdering Carolina.

How did she die? He wondered. *She was still breathing when I left her hotel suite. Why did I leave that room payment receipt on the desk? The cops must have seen it, they'll wonder why I paid her bill and left her alone when she was dying. I'll tell them it was a loan.*

At the police station

"Dan, Bradley Pickett has arrived, shall I send him in?" Midge asked. "He's as nervous as a cat."

"Hold off for twenty minutes, Midge. Let's let him sweat a while longer. If he's not guilty of murder, he's guilty of something."

After five minutes, Brad walked to Midge's desk. "I can't wait all day, how much longer is it going to be? Tell the detective he's got three minutes and then I'm out the door."

"I'd have a seat if I were you, Mr. Pickett," said Midge as she reached in her drawer and pulled out a pair of handcuffs. She had no intention of using them, but Brad didn't know that.

Brad scowled but did as he was told and waited silently until he was called into Detective North's office.

***

"Suppose you tell me what you were doing in Carolina Bloom's hotel suite the night she died."

"Carolina asked me to help her out. She was strapped for money until her royalty checks came in from California. The hotel was giving her a hard time for not paying her bill. I helped her out by covering for her."

"Ten-thousand dollars to be exact. You must be a particularly good friend."

"Not really, she and I had a little fling for old-time sake. You know what I mean. It was a loan; she'd planned to pay me back. I'll get it from her estate now."

"Mr. Pickett, have you had a rat problem in your New York apartment?"

"With the rent I pay, there'd better not be any rats. The rats stay away from the affluent areas. Is that why you left New York City, Detective? Was your apartment infested?" Brad said with a smirk.

"Mr. Pickett, there are rats throughout the city, even the two-legged kind."

Brad didn't know what to make of this cop. *What a stupid question to ask. I don't like his insinuation, is he calling me a rat?*

"Mr. Pickett, have you ever purchased or used rat poison?"

"What's all this talk about rats, and now it's poison. I didn't come all this way to talk about the rat problem in New York."

"Just answer the question, did you ever purchase or use rat poison?"

"No, I never have used rat poison or mouse poison or poison of any kind. If I find a fly in my apartment, I call maintenance to get rid of it. Now, if you will excuse me, I'm leaving."

"Mr. Pickett, are you aware Carolina Bloom ingested rat poison over time and died as a result?"

"Is that what made her sick?" Brad murmured. "I didn't know, I wondered why she hadn't called me in a few months."

"Mr. Pickett, is it true you spent time in the staff lounge at the television station where Ms. Bloom's show broadcasts?"

"I've been there, Carolina asked me to wait for her a few times while she was doing her show. Where else would I wait?"

"You were alone in the room, isn't that true?"

"Yes, I guess I was. The old bat, Barb, told me not to change the station, but I did anyway. That woman doesn't like me," Brad laughed.

"What do you know about the storage closet in that room?"

"Where is this leading, Detective? Do I need to call my lawyer?"

"That is your right, Mr. Pickett."

"I want this over. I know nothing about a closet, and I know nothing about Carolina's murder. I hated this town when I lived here, and I hate it more now. The sooner I can leave the happier I'll be."

"You are free to go, Mr. Pickett. I'll be in touch if we have more questions for you."

***

Brad almost flew out the door. He couldn't wait to get back to the city and call on the lovely Belinda, or Melinda, he couldn't remember her name.

"You let him go, Dan, I'd have guessed he was guilty of something," said Midge.

"He is guilty of something, but he didn't murder Carolina Bloom. The frat boy doesn't have the nerve to swat a fly. It's not my business, but he's hiding something that has nothing to do with this case."

Chapter Twenty-One

Most of the actors and behind-the-scenes volunteers gathered in the meeting room of the Community Playhouse. The buzz of voices could be heard as Detective North entered the room. He could only guess they were discussing the demise of their leading lady.

"Thank you for meeting with me today. Ms. Clark, is everyone involved with the Playhouse present, specifically during Carolina Bloom's stint?"

"All the regulars except Barry Kemp, who also works at the television station. Your assistant said you would interview him there. Also, Elaine Baker is visiting her daughter and new grandson in Philadelphia. She will return to Oakwood Park if necessary. We have several high school students who act as ushers for our performances. They weren't involved with Ms. Bloom. I can quickly put in a call to the principal if you feel you need to question them."

"I doubt that will be necessary. First, I want to assure you, folks, no one here is being accused of a crime. A woman has died and it's my job to find out why she died and who wanted Carolina Bloom dead."

"Detective North, if you ask me, everyone in this room had reason to dislike Carolina," said Harvey Rutledge. "However, there isn't a murderer among us. Have you considered Ms. Bloom died by her own hand? The woman was a drama queen, I wouldn't put it past her to stage her own death."

"Mr. Rutledge, that thought crossed my mind too. However, the doctor assures me the effects of the poison in her system caused her agony. There are less painful ways to commit suicide."

While the others waited, each person was interviewed in Sandy Clark's office. Rebecca, having been questioned before, was excused. She, however, stayed with the group to reassure them that Detective North was not the enemy. As each person left Sandy's office, they were escorted to the door. Harvey Rutledge was the last questioned.

"Golly, Detective, you took a chance I wouldn't keel over waiting for my turn. I'm an old man and I have little time left."

Dan laughed; he liked this old gentleman. "I'm not worried Mr. Rutledge, I think you will outlive us all.

"Tell me, do you have any idea who might be responsible for Carolina's murder?"

"Not a clue, the woman was a real pain in the backside. I hate to say it, but if she hadn't gotten sick when she did, I think we'd have lost most of our crew. I'd never heard so many complaints from our group as I did when the queen was around."

Detective North left the Playhouse more baffled than before. He liked the people of Oakwood Park and was glad he was now part of the community. When he was a kid, he liked to watch old cowboy movies with his dad. He pictured himself in a white hat saving the town single handedly. When this case was solved, maybe he'd audition for a part a play. Perhaps they'd let him wear a white hat.

Rebecca Snow called out to Dan as he was leaving the building.

"I'm sorry, Detective, did I startle you?"

"That's okay, I was daydreaming. Tell me, Mrs. Snow, are all the people involved with the Community Playhouse volunteers?"

"Sandy Clark receives a minimal salary, but the rest do it because they love the theater. Some like acting and others like all the behind-the-scenes activities. It's a good group of people. Harvey Rutledge is a retired drama teacher. We tell him Broadway missed out when he chose to stay in Oakwood Park.

"Why do you ask, Detective, are you interested in our playhouse?"

Dan North smiled, "Maybe," he said.

"Good, Sandy is always looking for people who have an interest in acting or working around the stage."

***

On the drive to the television station, Rebecca thought about her conversation with the detective. Someone like him would bring new life to the group. She thought he would be perfect for the part of Detective Turley. Barry Kemp wanted to play the detective, but he had stage fright when he'd been given a chance to act. Sandy couldn't take a chance on him.

A feeling she couldn't describe came over her. Carolina's death took a toll on Barry. Rebecca often wondered if Barry had a crush on Carolina. She remembered his excitement when he'd heard she was moving to Oakwood Park.

Carolina had to know Barry's feelings for her. She treated him with such disdain, ordering him around and ridiculing him when anyone else was within hearing distance. Barry was shy and withdrawn back in high school and that hadn't changed in all these years.

He was proud of his job at the station and happy to be involved in the playhouse. I think he enjoyed painting scenery and constructing sets. He seemed to have given up on acting. I can remember working alongside him, he couldn't take his eyes off Carolina.

I can't believe what I'm thinking, Barry Kemp is no more capable of murder than I am. Yet, I have an uneasy feeling in the pit of my stomach.

At the television station

"Barb, have you seen Barry Kemp today?"

"Not since he came early this morning, Rebecca. He might be in the basement with Hank. Barry often visits the maintenance man. They both are avid fisherman and talk about their latest catches. Do you need his help?"

"No, I simply wanted to talk to him. I'll find him."

"Oh, dear, I hope we aren't both having the same doubts about Barry."

"Why do you say that Barb?" Rebecca said with uneasiness in her voice.

"What happened to Carolina has me spooked. I'm letting my imagination work overtime. It's just that Carolina took every opportunity to belittle and shame Barry. I've been trying to ignore my suspicions; however, I think you are having those thoughts too."

"I'm afraid the thought has been in the back of my mind since the coroner reported his findings. I find it hard to believe Barry could do such a thing, but everyone has a breaking point. I could see the toll Carolina's abuse was taking on the poor man. She seemed to take pleasure in watching him squirm when she called him names. If only Barry had fought back but, he'd go out of his way to please her. It was hard to watch. I wish I'd spoken up, not that Carolina would have listened.

"Did you notice when Carolina began her sick leave? He was a different man, he was like the Barry I used to know, full of smiles and quietly content."

"I noticed," said Barb, "Although, the entire staff was in a better mood when you took over the morning show. Even I walked on eggshells around Carolina and you know what a tough old bird I can be.

"Detective North is due to arrive soon. He will talk to everyone individually; you and I have already been interviewed so we are off the hook. What happened with the Pickett fellow? Do you know if he's been questioned?"

"I don't know, Detective North doesn't offer information. That's a sign of a good detective but I would love to be a fly on the wall during that discussion. Brad Pickett is a jerk."

"He is a jerk but a handsome one. With Carolina's mean streak and Pickett's ego, those two were made for each other. Now, one of them is dead."

"I'm hoping Brad is the culprit too, however, if he were going to kill someone, he'd do it quickly.

Waiting patiently for Carolina to die doesn't fit with his personality."

Chapter Twenty-Two

Detective North gave Barb a list of those he wanted to interview. Barry Kemp's name was listed first.

"Detective, Barry Kemp is involved in a project, I'd hate to stop him in the middle, is it all right if the folks on this list are called out of order?"

"That will be fine, Ms. Tinsdale," the detective said giving her a suspicious look.

***

Meanwhile, Rebecca searches for Barry. Hank is busy running a sweeper in the staff lounge.

"Hank, have you seen Barry this morning?"

"No, Mrs. Snow, I haven't seen him all morning. Maybe he's with Ms. Tinsdale, he likes her."

"No, I just came from Ms. Tinsdale's office, she hasn't seen him either."

"When he gets anxious, he sometimes goes into the supply room in the basement. He used to hide there often when Ms. Bloom was still here. I'm sorry the woman is dead, but no one around here is mourning her loss. I know that's not nice to say, but Hank Gardener always tells it like it is."

"I know that about you, Hank and it's a good quality to have. We need more folks like you who tell the truth. I'm sure you never let Ms. Bloom get under your skin as Barry did."

"No, she didn't get under my skin, but I knew better than to talk back to her. You know, Mr. Carlson really liked her…I mean…really liked her. I heard Mrs. Carlson in his office giving him what for after everyone in the administration office left one night."

"Hank, I've never known Mrs. Carlson to come to the station, are you certain it was her?"

"Oh, yes, Ma'am, it was Mrs. Carlson all right. I like to do most of my work at night when the place is vacant and when folks aren't hanging around making messes and raising dust. Mrs. Carlson comes in late at night and snoops through Mr. Carlson's files. Usually, Mr. Carlson is gone when she comes in."

"Usually, do you mean he was still in the office the time you heard them arguing?"

"Yes, and he wasn't alone."

"Hank, was Carolina with Mr. Carlson that night?"

"I've said too much already. I don't know if it was Ms. Bloom, but I saw a blonde lady running down the hallway from Mr. Carlson's office. Her hair was disheveled, and she was carrying her shoes. It could have been Ms. Bloom, but I didn't see her face."

"Hank, is the supply room door normally locked?"

"No, it never is. I don't think there is a key to the door. There is nothing of value in the room. If I'm not here, the staff can get in there if they need anything. I'd guess there aren't many who know the storeroom exists."

"Obviously, Barry Kemp knows of its existence."

"Yes, Barry likes to help me when things are slow upstairs. He's a nice fellow although he's very timid."

"Do you mind if I look for him in the basement?"

"No, not at all. Something has been bothering the lad for the last couple of days. Maybe he cared more for Ms. Bloom than I realized, although I don't know why."

"Hank, do you know if rat poison is kept in the storeroom?"

"Hmm, we had a problem with a rat about two years ago. I think there was only one, but Mr. Carlson was afraid there could be more moving in. He had me order a box of poison pellets. Oh my, you don't suppose those pellets were used to kill Ms. Bloom?"

***

The basement was dark and damp. Rebecca was sorry she hadn't brought along a sweater. She spotted a closed door and assumed it was the storeroom. She gingerly knocked on the door and called Barry's name. There was no answer.

"Barry," she called again, "Barry, it's Rebecca Snow, are you in there?"

The door slowly opened; Barry peeked out the crack. "Are you alone, Rebecca?"

"Yes, Barry, may I come in?"

Barry opened the door wide enough for Rebecca to enter and then closed it again.

"How did you know I was here? Did Hank tell you about this room? Nobody else knows I come here sometimes."

"Yes, Barry, Hank said you might be here. I'm worried about you."

Rebecca looked around the darkened room. The only light was from a small window on the left wall. She spotted a box on a shelf and recognized the skull and crossbones image. Her heart sank, Barry is one of the few people who knew about this room. He must have known the rat poison was here. If her instincts were correct, Barry did indeed commit murder.

"Barry do you want to talk?" Rebecca asked.

"It's my fault, Rebecca, Carolina died because of me."

Rebecca realized this wasn't a confession of murder, is it possible Carolina's death was an accident?

"Barry, tell me what happened. I think it will make you feel better to talk about it."

"It was late one night after Mr. Carlson had gone home. Carolina was extra mean to me that day, and I hid in here until she'd left the building. She called me a mole and said I should live underground with the worms. I asked her why she wanted to hurt my feelings and she laughed, 'go back under the bridge, troll' she said.

"I fell asleep down here, and didn't wake up until I heard footsteps. I could tell the person was wearing high heels, and I thought it was Carolina and she was coming to taunt me again. I hid in the broom closet and peeked through a crack in the door. It wasn't Carolina, it was Mrs. Carlson. I saw her reach for the rat poison. She poured pellets into a plastic bag and left the room turning off the light and closing the door. It was so dark I couldn't see a thing. I waited until I heard a car start in the parking lot and felt my way out of the room and to the stairs. I was afraid I'd be in trouble if Mrs. Carlson told Mr. Carlson that I was asleep in the basement.

"I didn't understand why Mrs. Carlson wouldn't call an exterminator if she had a rat problem. I was so happy not to be caught I put it out of my mind until I heard the reason Carolina died and it was my fault."

"Barry, it wasn't your fault. If the rat poison Mrs. Carlson took off the shelf that night was used to kill Carolina, it had nothing to do with you. Detective North is interviewing everyone as we speak. You must tell him what you know."

"I can't, Rebecca, Mr. Carlson will be mad if I tell the police."

"Barry, my son is a lawyer. If Mr. Carlson fires you, he will represent you and you will keep your job." Rebecca didn't know if Alex could save Barry's job, but she had to persuade him to tell the truth.

***

"Detective North, Barry Kemp has some important information about the Bloom murder. He is reluctant to tell his story for fear of losing his job," said Rebecca.

"Don't worry, Mrs. Snow, I'm accustomed to reluctant witnesses, I won't bite his head off, I promise."

Detective North was true to his word. He didn't bite Barry's head off; he was very compassionate in his questioning.

Barry relaxed enough to tell the same story he'd told Rebecca.

***

"I think the detective believed me, Rebecca, he said it wasn't my fault that Carolina died. I feel so much better although I'm sorry I was happy when she was so sick, she couldn't come to work. Carolina was a good actress, wasn't she?"

"Yes, Barry, she was a better actress than we thought. I don't believe she meant to be mean to you, she simply didn't know how to be nice."

Chapter Twenty-Three

At the Carlson Home

A haughty gentleman dressed in a perfectly fitted jacket, vest and striped trousers complete with white gloves answered the door.
The look on his face told Detective North the service entrance was on the other side of the mansion.

"Good morning, Jeeves, I'm here to speak to Mrs. Carlson," Dan said showing his badge.

"Sir, my name is not Jeeves and Mrs. Carlson are resting."

"I'd suggest you wake her up, Claude, unless you want to be hauled to the jailhouse for interfering with police business."

"Who is it Charles, who is at the door?"

"Mrs. Harriet Carlson?" Dan flashed his badge again and introduced himself. "I have a few questions about the murder of Carolina Bloom."

"Mabel, call Alfred Dunkirk. Detective, I have nothing to say without my attorney present."

"That is your right, Ma'am. I am arresting you on suspicion of the murder of Carolina Bloom. You have the right to remain silent, you have the right..."

"I'm well aware of my rights, Detective. I refuse to budge from this house."

"Cuff her, Detective Granger. Mabel, tell Mrs. Carlson's lawyer to meet her at the police station."

"You can't put those things on me, I'll go with you, but don't you dare touch me or I'll sue the police department, the mayor and the city."

Detective Granger took great pleasure in taking Mrs. Carlson's arm and escorting her to the detective's car. Dan smiled as he activated the blue flashing lights of the car alerting the snooty Mrs. Carlson's neighbors of her arrest.

***

"Barb, I have to leave, cancel my appointments for the rest of the day. My wife is under arrest for the murder of Carolina Bloom."

Barb's sense of relief that Barry Kemp was not a suspect in the murder was almost overwhelming. She called Rebecca's cell phone immediately.

"I knew he didn't do it," she shouted into the phone when Rebecca answered.

"Barry is a relieved young man. He is giving his official statement to the police now. They brought Mrs. Carlson in; she looks like a madwoman instead of the high-society person she pretends to be. How is Mr. Carlson taking it?"

"He's in shock, I think he's worried about his own skin, I doubt she'll let him keep his cushy job after this. Is it true, Rebecca, did the old bat knock off Carolina?"

"It looks that way, the evidence is mostly circumstantial unless Mrs. Carlson confesses, she'll probably get away with murder."

"I suppose the motive is jealousy, Mr. Carlson has an eye for the ladies. That's one reason Mrs. Carlson lets me keep my job, she knows I'm not a threat to her marriage."

"That's because you have better taste in men than Mr. Carlson," Rebecca said with a chuckle.

Mabel took her time calling Mrs. Carlson's attorney. She was tired of the woman's browbeating. Mabel had worked for Harriet Carlson for twenty-five years and was treated no better than the upstairs maid.

Last week she'd withheld her pay because Mabel was fifteen minutes late getting to work because of a traffic accident on the highway that held up traffic.

***

"Where's my attorney, Angus, he should be here by now? Call Mabel and find out what the holdup is," Harriet demanded.

"Harriet, did you hurt Carolina? You can tell me, I'm your husband, they can't make me testify against you."

"Yes, I did it. She wasn't supposed to die but good riddance to the little tramp. I saw her in your office that night, half-dressed and you with lipstick all over your face. She flew out of the room when she heard me coming. It was the night you and I were to celebrate our thirtieth anniversary and I catch you romping around with another woman. You said you forgot about our dinner plans. We had a terrible fight, and that's when I decided to teach the blonde hussy a lesson.
"If I didn't check all your expenditures, I never would have known about the rat poison you bought two years ago."

"Rat poison, how would you know about rat poison? I don't remember telling you about finding a rat in the basement."

"You didn't, you fool, do you think I trust you with my money? I know every penny you have spent for the last ten years.
"I figured the poison would still be in the storeroom because I know you throw nothing away. I poured a few pellets into a plastic bag and left the box there. They can't prove I touched the box because I wore gloves.

"I didn't intend for the trollop to die, I wanted her to be sick enough to lose her looks. I scraped the pellets and just put a sprinkling of the poison in Carolina's pineapple juice. I knew she made Barb order that special juice. Barb doesn't lock her desk drawer when she leaves at night, I check up on her too.

"After Rebecca took over the morning show, I knew Carolina would pack her bags and leave town. Rebecca was much more popular than Carolina and the sponsors stopped complaining about the content of the show.

"I thought Carolina would recover and there wouldn't be any need to keep her feeling sick. She was a weakling, that small amount of poison wouldn't have killed a stronger person."

"Harriet, how could you deliberately make another human being suffer?"

"What about the suffering she caused me, Carolina was trying to steal my husband? She thought you were rich but didn't know I'm the one with the money and I don't plan to loosen those purse strings again."

"Harriet, you have confessed to the murder of Carolina Bloom and I have recorded your confession. I'm divorcing you; Harriet and I will gladly testify against you in a court of law. Oh, you are allowed one phone call, I suggest you make that call to your attorney. Mabel ended her employment and refused to follow your orders to call him."

Harriet's shrieks could be heard throughout the hallways of the first floor of the police station.

"Sounds like you solved your case, Detective Dan," said Midge.

"I wish I could take the credit, but it was Rebecca Snow who convinced Barry Kemp to tell what he knew. I don't know if we could have made the charges stick if it hadn't been for Angus Carlson. I think he was in love with Carolina Bloom. Considering all I've heard about Ms. Bloom; she wasn't the easiest person to love."

"Compared to his wife, I'd say she was a vast improvement," laughed Midge.

Epilogue

Harriet Carlson

"Alfred, I want to divorce Angus before he can divorce me. Draw up the papers and get them finalized," said Harriet Carlson while scratching her leg where the ankle monitor irritates her skin.

"Harriet, as your attorney, I must insist you let Angus file for divorce. He'll take you for everything you have if you do it first."

"He wouldn't dare. I wish you could convince the judge to get this thing off me."

"You can always sit in a jail cell until your case goes to trial."

Harriet sneered at the older man. If her daddy were still alive, he'd get her out of this mess. Where was Mabel when she needed her? Charles left her too. Wasn't anyone loyal to her?

Alfred did as she asked. He was relieved when Angus said he wanted nothing more than the television station. He wasn't asking for alimony or division of property.

"No, he can't have the station, I won't allow it," Harriet shouted.

"Harriet, the station will be sold if you are sent to prison, I told you that is a strong possibility. This house will be sold, and the money put into a trust for when you are free. Angus is entitled to half of everything you own, be glad he's only asking for the station."

Reluctantly, Harriet signed the television station over to her soon-to-be ex-husband.

Three months later she was found guilty of second-degree murder and sentenced to fifteen years in a women's penitentiary.

Angus Carlson

"Alfred, I don't care about Harriet's money, she held that over me for our entire married life. I'll walk away from the marriage with nothing if that's what it takes to set me free. I would, however, like to request ownership of the television station. Without Harriet's interference, I think my staff and I can make it the best local station for miles around."

"Angus, I'll present your offer to Harriet and with some persuasion, I trust she will agree."

As the owner of the television station, Angus turned over a new leaf. He rented a small apartment a block from his office and spent most of his time improving and working toward his goal to make the station shine.

He took Barry Kemp under his wing and promoted him with the idea he would eventually take over the daily operation.

Everyone who worked at the station could see the change in their boss. He generously raised their salaries and increased their vacation days. The turnover in the department was almost non-existent. It was now a happy place to work and Carolina Bloom was nothing but an unpleasant memory.

Detective Daniel North

Detective North kept the promise he'd made to himself and talked to Sandy Clark about volunteering at the Community Playhouse. He found he enjoyed acting the part of the culprit in a murder mystery.

His partner, Rob Granger accepted a job in Chicago. Dan tried to convince Rebecca that with her sleuthing skills she should apply at the academy.

"No, Dan, I'll let the younger women do that, I have my hands full with the show and the playhouse and my family now that everyone is home again."

***

"You need a partner and there is a perfect one for you," said Midge.

"You, Midge, that would be great."

"Not me, I like my job. I'm talking about the young woman who just walked through the door."

Dan looked up to see a brunette with flashing brown eyes staring back at him. She looked and walked like a fashion model.

"Who's that?"

"Your new partner Erica West, the captain thought it would be fun to have Detectives North and West working together," chuckled Midge.

Bradley Pickett

Brad sipped his favorite brand of scotch looking out his apartment window at the flashing lights of the city below.

He laughed when he read about the snooty Harriet Carlson's conviction in the murder of Carolina Bloom. He didn't care who knocked Carolina off as long as she was out of his life.

Brad was expecting the lovely Angelina. He was on top of the world, Carolina was out of his life, he'd made another killing in the market, this time it was almost legitimate, and he was waiting for a beauty who would make his night perfect.

The doorbell rang. He hurried to the door opened it and heard the words:

"FBI…Bradley Albert Pickett, you are under arrest for securities fraud and insider trading."

Coming Soon:

Murder at Bradbury Hill
A Rebecca Snow Cozy Mystery

Elderly twin sisters, Anna and Emma Bradbury, owners of the home on Bradbury Hill, are found dead because of carbon monoxide poisoning.

The prime suspect is Jake Morgan, fiancé of Mackenzie Snow and long-time friend of the Snow family. Jake is an accountant at a reputable accounting firm in Oakwood Park. As a favor to the sisters, Jake visits their home weekly to help them pay their bills and keep them company.

Jake's recent bank loan for twenty-five thousand dollars is paid in full close to the time of the twins' death. Jake refuses to disclose the reason for the loan and the swift repayment.

Despite Rebecca Snow's protests, Detectives Daniel North and Erica West are certain they have found their man.

Rebecca and her daughter, Mackenzie, are determined to uncover the truth and clear Jake's name.

9 798869 380985 7